*Praise for Sharp as a Serp.*

"*Mandy Haynes' writing voice is as smooth as fabled Tennessee whiskey. And she's a Southern front porch story- teller. The back porch is for those who wander all over the place and never get a good story told, them that don't know what's boring and what's not. Mandy knows good stories and this collection, SHARP AS A SERPENT'S TOOTH, like her first, WALKING THE WRONG WAY HOME, proves her top shelf skill as a writer and gives readers more than they came for.*" —Sonny Brewer, author of The Poet of Tolstoy Park, and other novels.

"*Mandy Haynes pushes us into the carnival tents of holy roller snake oil barkers wielding serpents against the hearts of innocents who see their nakedness. She shows us preach- ers both benevolent and malevolent. She places us behind the eyes of girls who chunk rocks and aim arrows at bad guys who might once have taken them in, but who figure it out and serve up just desserts. It's no wonder such a young woman might be enthralled with a guitar strumming rebel who tan- gles with a serpent handler. This is a slithering snake pit of gothic tales that rattle and hiss with the truth we don't always like to see.*"
—Joe Formichella, multiple literary award winner, Push- cart Prize nominee, finalist for a New Letters Literary Prize, and author of five works of fiction, including Pulpwood Queen International Book Club pick *Waffle House Rules* and three works of nonfiction, including Foreword magazine's book of the year/true crime *Murder Creek*

*"Like the best songwriters, Mandy crafts her stories with people and places you can recognize, especially those of us from the South! Just like a great song, it's the details that get you...some that are written and some that are only implied."* —Tammy Rogers-King, Grammy award winning singer/songwriter/musician

*"Mandy Haynes captures the authentic southern stories readers love. She writes, not with stereotypes readers can spot from a mile away, but with wisdom which comes from the calloused hands of a great author."* —Renea Winchester, author of Outbound Train.

*"Mandy Haynes writes about the poor and damaged, about simple folks with fire and crazy pulsing through their veins. In the story "Eva" she displays the ugly drippings of an evil soul beside the strength and wisdom of a child. With a warped sense of humor and an eye for sweet revenge, Haynes, in her collection of short stories "Sharp as a Serpent's Tooth," reveals herself to be an emerging talent with a command of southern dialogue and a tendency to create dirt-under-the-fingernails characters. She'll be around for the long haul."* —Brenda Sutton Rose, author of *Dogwood Blues*, nominated for 2015 Georgia Author of the Year for First Novel, nominated for a 2018 Pushcart Prize in Fiction for her short story "Samuel's Wife".

*"With an ear for conversation and a storyteller's gift, Mandy spins tales of ordinary peoples' struggles that are both touching and compelling."* —Richard Bailey (otherwise known #3)

# SHARP
# AS A
# SERPENT'S
# TOOTH

## Eva and other stories

Mandy Haynes

*Dedicated to my nieces Kaili, Delaini, Baili, Savannah, Lily and Emma, my great niece Paisley, and my granddaughter Ruby Kate*

*May you all become strong independent women who know your worth and have your own stories to tell.*

"Rule number one. If it ain't yours, don't touch it."
Laurel, The Day I Threw the Rock


"Be wise as serpents, innocent as doves."
Jesus, Matthew 10:16

Eva..............................................................................1

Plans for Sweet Lorraine........................................73

The Day I Threw the Rock.....................................95

Junebug Fischer....................................................109

Cussing Snakes and Candy Cigarettes..................191

# Eva

*"Behold, you give unto me the power to tread on serpents, and over all the power of the enemy, and nothing shall by any means hurt me..."*

Before the Elliotts came to our town, with their big canvas tent and wooden crates that smelled of mold and stagnant pond water, we had our regular service on Sunday in the little church on the square. I never even wondered if there was another way to worship or that people had different ways of interpreting the bible. Brother Talley's sermons were all I'd ever known.

He started preaching the same year I was born. He was twenty-three then, and thirty-four when the Elliotts showed up, so he was as much a part of this town as the coal mines and moonshine stills up in the mountains. You can't imagine one without the other. Every Sunday morning, Brother Talley preached out of the white steepled building from nine in the morning until ten or so. His sermons were long enough to get in the required amount of hallelujahs and amens, or if you asked my daddy, long enough to get an invite for dinner. Which he got lots of because everyone loved Brother Talley.

Well, almost everyone. There were the old timers who didn't like the fact that he'd been seen some Saturday mornings coming from the widow Flannery's house, but that was just gossip Mama said, and nobody's business when I asked her why that seemed to make people upset.

"For Pete's sake, Delene, go play and mind your own business. You make my ears tired," was actually how she put it.

There were a few women who didn't like the fact that Brother Talley kept a flask in his back pocket. Daddy told me he needed it to keep his vocal chords flexible for all the preaching he did on Sunday and that we shouldn't judge others. Both of my parent's answers felt right, even if I thought Mama's answer was a little rude.

And he was handsome, too. I have to admit, the summer I turned sixteen I had myself a little crush—but that's another story for another day.

Regardless of what he did on Friday nights or the corn liquor in his back pocket, no one could argue that Brother Talley was the first to help out if someone was in trouble. No matter what your problems were, if you needed help with a new roof on your barn or a hand to hold when a loved one passed, he was there with that smile of his and a strong shoulder to lean on. And his sermons were as upbeat as he was. He would preach about salvation, about giving, and hope, and about the promise of a better place for all of us. He was always complimenting the ladies and making them blush, patting the men on the back and making them stand a little taller. He wanted everyone to be proud of themselves and to be the best they could be.

Every Sunday the people sitting in the pews would be dressed in their nicest clothes—even if their best was only their patched-up work clothes. Heck, we were just an old mining town that had seen better days –but on Sundays, Brother Talley made everybody feel like we lived in paradise. It didn't matter if you mined, farmed, or worked downtown in a fancy office like my daddy, according to him we were all equal and we were all loved.

Reverend Elliott had other ways of preaching. We found out soon after he and his wife rolled into town that we weren't nothing but a bunch of heathens headed straight to hell—with Satan himself nippin' at our heels. Why, the way we dressed was an abomination in itself! Not to mention the tobacco in the fellas' pockets or the beards that so many of the men had on their faces. Nothing but a bunch of low-down, shameful sinners. They didn't even care to know about all the good things everyone did for each other. They judged us by the way we looked and that was it. If what Reverend Elliott said was true, our parents would be the first in line for the fiery pits of hell, with all their dancing and carrying on. Shoot, Old Scratch would make Daddy a foreman!

13

But when we overheard our parents from our hiding place in the stairwell talking about the Elliotts, our worries were put to rest. If my parents felt comfortable poking fun and making good natured jokes about the way the Reverend preached and his stern, bible-thumping wife, then we had nothing to be worried about.

Besides, Mama was just too dang nice to go to hell.

But those two, the Reverend and his wife, seemed determined to save all of our poor, lost souls. In less than a week, they brought their show right into town and started talking their talk. They set up shop on the corner by the post office and you could find them there every day a week.

They appeared to be on a mission.

"I'm a soldier in the army of the Lord," the Reverend's wife would shout, raising her arms above her head as she marched back and forth in front of her husband, repeating the phrase again and again.

"If I sing, let me sing in the army of the Lord, if I preach, let me preach in the army of the Lord, if I die, let me die in the army of the Lord." She'd stop to shout when she needed a break from marching.

Her husband called down from his store-bought stepping stool, "You must be devout and a warrior for Christ! You must come to church prepared to wage spiritual warfare against the devil!"

Their voices were loud and clear, with particular emphasis on the "I" and "T" in Christ. It sounded like they were talking through a megaphone, but they weren't. Their booming voices reminded me of the men at the carnival that set up every summer in the next town over. The men who would get you to spend all your pennies trying to win some stuffed animal you didn't even want, or a poor, half-dead goldfish in a plastic bag. If you listened long enough you would dig down in your pocket, find your last five cents and hand it over in exchange for three wooden balls you knew weren't heavy enough to knock down the weighted bottles stacked up on the platform four feet away. Even though you knew better. The carnies had a way about them, just like the Elliotts. But I couldn't figure out what they were peddling.

The two of them were a sight to see, Mr. Elliott with that slicked back, greasy hair, standing on the stool in a suit that didn't quite fit, and Mrs. Elliott in her plain, brown dress, waving her arms above her head. Even if it was disturbing, you couldn't help but stop and watch.

It was like looking at Mr. Pratt's old bull, Big Bill, in his pasture on the way to school. Hank said that if he really wanted to, Big Bill could charge right through his fence and put his horns in you. Stick them clean through.

It made the hair on the back of your neck stand on end and made your stomach flutter. But if he was close enough, without being too close, you couldn't help but stop and stare.

That's how it felt for me staring at the Elliotts on the corner, but there wasn't even a rickety fence between us.

* * *

Mama and Daddy had Brother Talley over for dinner a few days after the Elliotts arrived. It seemed like they were all everyone talked about since they'd showed up and it didn't look they were leaving any time soon. Along with the regular talk came some unsettling gossip.

The day before, someone came into the bank and told my daddy that Reverend Elliott was going to take over the church. I know because I was playing in the stairwell when Daddy came home from work and told Mama. I happened to overhear them in the kitchen even though I wasn't eavesdropping that time. Mama made a joke, which was her usual response when she was anxious, and started making plans for the next night's dinner.

"Well, if there is anything to the rumors—which I'm sure there isn't—we'll find out tomorrow night. I've never known Talley to turn down a home-cooked meal," she said.

Mama was right. Brother Talley showed up at five o'clock on the dot the next night. After he said grace, he reassured my folks that no one was trying to take over his church. He scooped up a big spoonful of mashed potatoes and beamed at us.

"There's no need to worry, the Elliotts just feel like our town needs a boost, that we need to get a little closer to the spirit is how they put it," he said with a slight chuckle. "I'm intrigued by their, uhm, enthusiasm and looking forward to going to one of their sermons. I hope that the whole town will make them feel welcome and show them how neighborly we are."

Over Mama's blackberry cobbler we learned they were setting up a tent and would have their service a week from Wednesday.

"A tent?" Hank and I asked at the same time.

"Yep, a tent." Brother Talley replied with that grin of his that seemed to always be in the corners of his mouth. It was tucked under two deep dimples that never quite smoothed out and gave him a boyish look.

"Why don't they use the church?" Hank asked.

"Well, it's called a tent revival. I reckon they'd have to re-name it if they used our church." He chuckled, then went on to explain in a more serious voice. "They travel around from place to place to preach to people who live in places that don't have a church. The tent can be moved around and set up to make a temporary place to worship. I guess they feel more comfortable using it."

I thought of how the Elliotts made me think of the people that ran the carnival. I almost made a joke but I wasn't sure if Mama would think it was funny. Especially in front of Brother Talley, so I kept it to myself.

He took a second helping of cobbler and said, "I have to admit I'm curious. In more ways than one." He cut his eyes at Daddy, "They're setting up on the Carnton's property."

"The Carnton's don't even go to..." Hank started to say, but Mama shushed him quick.

"You don't say." Daddy said, hiding a grin. "Well, we'll be there." Mr. Carnton was a mean old cuss and a little bit crazy. He and Daddy had a history. When my daddy was a little boy, Mr. Carnton chased him down the creek with a shotgun. Daddy had just been fishing, but Mr. Carnton was convinced he worked for the DEA. He still does, which Daddy gets a kick out of.

"Well, it can't hurt anything I guess." Mama said.

"Who knows? It might do us all some good. If we never look

at other ways of doing something, how do we know that we're doing it the right way?" Brother Talley replied.

We finished our dessert and Hank and I helped Mama clean up the kitchen while the men went out to the porch for a smoke.

Hank was a great big brother. He always kept me informed on things that my parents or other adults thought I was too young to hear. Like the time Lester Cobb cut his finger off at the sawmill and they packed it on ice in Lester's lunch pail to take to Doctor Gentry to sew back on. Hank said Lester ate his near frozen ham biscuit while they stitched him up.

It wasn't that I didn't have friends, but they weren't interested in the things I liked to do. I would rather spend my time with Hank, but he was four years older than me and had a girl he was sweet on. It seemed like the only time we were together anymore was when we were doing chores.

* * *

As the days passed, we heard more and more about the Elliotts. They were making their rounds and spreading the word, inviting everyone out to worship with them in a few days. I'd taken to walking past them on the corner at least once a day.

I'd slow down as I passed but never had the nerve to stop—afraid they would point me out for eavesdropping or worse. I felt like a blasphemous heathen because I would take everything I heard back home and make jokes to Hank, putting on a show that would cause my brother to laugh himself silly. But one afternoon

I overheard Reverend Elliott referring to himself as a person of the Holy Ghost.

Well, that caught my ear and caused chill bumps to pop up clear down to my toes. I found myself standing right there in front, listening to every word.

I immediately started asking questions to anyone who would give me a minute to talk. I got most of my information from Mama Gladys, who wasn't any relation to us, or anyone else that I knew of. She owned the store where I'd trade sweeping her doorway for ropes of licorice. She knew everything about everything.

Daddy said that's why she never married.

Mama Gladys told me that being a person of the Holy Ghost meant you weren't scared to handle snakes, because you believed your faith in God would protect you from getting bitten. That you spoke in tongues, which wasn't really a language it was the spirit running through you. That you could cure diseases, cast out demons, and even drink lye or use fire on your skin and not get injured.

"Pick up snakes? Drink lye? Burn yourself on purpose? Why would anyone want to do that? I think that being able to cure disease and cast out demons sounds like fun—but drinking poison or handling snakes?" I asked Mama Gladys across the counter. "That's crazy talk."

Mama Gladys laughed, "Delene, girl, you're a mess."

I couldn't figure out what was so funny. I was dead serious, but I didn't get a chance to ask. Miss Stella came in with a basket of eggs for sale and a whole month's worth of gossip, so Mama Gladys told me I should come back another day.

I thought about what she'd told me on the walk home. Why would anyone want to pick up a snake? That didn't make sense to me. I tried to tell Mama what I'd heard, but she was fussing over a pan of fried chicken.

"That's the most ridiculous thing I've ever heard, Delene. Go outside and play, your imagination wears me out." She scooted me out of the kitchen without giving me a chance to ask her anything else. I stopped Daddy as he was coming up the walk.

"Daddy why would someone think that picking up a snake would make them closer to God?"

He stopped walking, but he was reading the newspaper and never even looked at me.

"That's a good question, hon." Then he walked past without giving me an answer. At the dinner table I tried again.

"Why would someone drink poison and burn themselves?"

"Delene, where are you coming up with this stuff?" Daddy asked.

"I'm not making it up. I swear. Reverend Elliott said they were Holy Spirits or something. Mama Gladys said…"

"Oh, that old hen." He held up his hands and laughed. "No wonder. Listen, kiddo. You need to quit hanging around the store so much or else people will start calling you Mama Dee."

Everyone laughed except me.

Mama, tired of hearing gossip and dodging my questions, came up with an idea.

"How about we invite the Elliotts over for dinner?" she asked Daddy. "We'll share a meal and have a nice conversation and get to know them. I'm sure that people are letting their imaginations get the best of them."

Daddy didn't answer right away.

Mama said, "It's the only way to know if the talk going around holds any truth."

"What talk?" I asked.

"They're trying to run Talley out of town." Hank answered before Mama could stop him.

"Wha…"

"Honey, it's just gossip. Don't worry about it." Mama made a face at Hank, but he acted like he didn't see it.

"It's not gossip, it's true." He said before taking a bite of his drumstick.

"What's true?" I asked.

Mama sighed and gave Daddy a different look. One he knew better than to ignore.

"Okay. I'll go by the corner tomorrow and invite them if that'll make everybody feel better. And stop some of this talk." Daddy looked at Hank, then me, and then Mama. She didn't notice, she had started planning what she was going to cook.

That night before bed I went to Hank's room and asked him what he'd meant about them trying to run Brother Talley out of town.

"Don't tell Mama I told you, Delene, but some money came up missing that was set aside for a new roof on the church."

"How did you hear that?" I asked.

"Everybody's talking at the sawmill. Aaron told me all about it, said Reverend Elliott was the one spreading the rumor. He came down there himself and told them to look at their preacher."

21

"Why would anybody think that Brother Talley would steal money? He doesn't even own a car or wear fancy clothes – what would he spend it on?"

"The question I want answered, is how Reverend Elliott knew about it. You know dang good and well if money came up missing, Mrs. Howard would've said something."

Mrs. Howard was the church's secretary and a know it all. She was one of the ones who didn't like Brother Talley having a flask and made comments about how widow Flannery dressed. If she thought Brother Talley was up to no good, she would've told everybody herself.

"I think they're trying to stir up trouble." Hank said.

"But why?" I asked.

"Think about it Delene. If Brother Talley wasn't here, then all of our tithes would go in their offering plate."

The Elliotts accepted the invitation and Mama made her famous chicken and dumplings with turnip greens and biscuits. For dessert she made a dozen fried apple pies with the apples we had canned the fall before. Mama loved to cook for company, no matter who it was.

That night she wore her best Sunday dress, even though it was only Tuesday, and made me wear a Sunday dress too. She wore her mother's brooch and made me put a ribbon that matched the color of my dress in my hair. The last thing she did to get me ready was to pinch my cheeks to make them pink.

She even made Daddy and Hank wear neckties and told us all to be on our best behavior. We didn't have time to argue too much, because the Reverend and his wife showed up ten minutes early.

I heard the loud knock at the door and ran to peer out through the parlor window. I wanted to get a good look at them before they came inside because I knew I would be too scared to look at them across the table. I was ready to take in every detail of the Reverend and his wife to use later to make Hank laugh, but a bright flash of orange stole my attention and I didn't see anything except a scrawny red-haired girl wedged in between them.

Daddy opened the door and let them in. I walked into the foyer and stood behind Mama, curious to find out who the girl was. She didn't look like either one of the adults she was standing with.

You could've knocked me down with the thump of a finger when I learned the girl was their daughter. No one had ever mentioned her before, and I'd never seen her with her parents on the square.

I tried not to stare, but I'd never seen anyone with golden eyelashes before. She was looking down at her feet, so her thick, light colored eyelashes seemed to glow against her skin. The skin on her face and neck was so pale that you could see the blue veins underneath, and her ears looked slightly pink, reminding me of the inside of a conch shell Daddy found one summer down in Gulf Shores.

The girl's dress was made of faded brown wool. I spied a pin holding the seam together at the waist and another one at the seam on her shoulder. She was so thin that I bet she could hide behind a sunflower stalk.

I put a hand up to one of my plump, glowing cheeks and felt it turn from pink to red. I felt like I was showing off just standing there dressed in a petticoat with a green ribbon in my hair and I wanted to run in my room and change.

Mrs. Elliott was dressed as plain as her daughter. She was big, built like a man, with broad shoulders and a wide face. Her eyebrows were thicker than Daddy's and I noticed one long whisker poking out of a mole on her chin as stiff as a broom bristle.

Until then, I hadn't really gotten a good look at her face. She was always moving, marching up and down the corner in front of her husband and calling out to the adults who passed by. She was even scarier standing still and being quiet.

She took one look at my mother in her pretty lavender dress with the lace collar and grimaced. A hateful look that caused her thin lips to disappear and her double chin to make a third row. I would've giggled at the face she made if it hadn't been so disturbing. If Mama noticed, I couldn't tell, but I could feel the dislike coming off the big woman in waves.

Daddy introduced his family to the Elliotts, then the Reverend did the same. Their daughter's name was Eva.

I put out my hand to shake hers, exactly like the grown-ups did, but she kept her hands in the folds of the rough, brown wool of her skirt and her eyes on the floor. I wasn't sure what to do next, but Mama came to my rescue and ushered everyone into the dining room.

Eva sat across the table from me, so it was hard not to stare at her as she ate. She was so quiet, you never even heard her fork touch her plate or anything. And she was so small that she barely took up any space, using only one hand the entire time. Eva never looked up once.

Mr. Elliot was doing most of the talking, but it wasn't about anything interesting. He went on about all the different places they'd preached while Mrs. Elliot picked at her plate like she was looking for a worm in her dumplings. She hadn't said anything to Mama even though Mama had tried to start a conversation several times. When it was clear no one was going to ask what having the holy spirit meant, or ask about poison or snakes, I asked to be excused.

"Would you like to come outside with me?" I asked Eva.

She didn't answer. She just looked up into her mother's stern face.

"Don't stray far, Eva. We will be ready to go shortly." There was a look in her mother's eyes that gave me a shiver. There was a smell, too, that I didn't like coming from her skin. It smelled like sulfur or burnt oil and gasoline. Like rotten eggs and old tractor parts. Something bad.

I reached out to take Eva's hand, but it was wrapped in her skirt, so I motioned for her to follow me instead and went out the back door after Hank. I figured it was a nervous habit or something, the way she fiddled with her skirt, like how Hank used to chew his nails until Mama threatened to put tabasco sauce on them. I couldn't blame Eva, I would be nervous too if my mama was so mean.

"So, where are you from?" I asked her as soon as we stepped

onto the back porch. I wanted to know everything. She raised her shoulders but didn't speak.

"Do you have any brothers or sisters?" Still no reply.

"How old are you?" I asked.

"I'm thirteen." Eva said in a voice not much louder than a whisper.

"Why, you ain't big as a minute. I'm almost twelve and kinda small for my size," I said, trying to make her laugh, but she didn't say anything else. Actually, I was only eleven and I was a whole head taller than her.

When we got close to the springhouse I stopped short and put my arm out in front of Eva.

"You have to be careful around this part of the yard, because of snakes." I said.

That got Eva's attention.

"What kind of snakes?" she asked, looking me straight in the eye for the first time. I was shocked at the color of her eyes. They were the prettiest shade of green I'd ever seen.

"Big ones," I said.

I will never forget how her eyes hooked onto me, like an electric current ran from her to me all the way down to my feet and out the bottom of my shoes into the packed dirt of the path. She must've felt it too because she smiled at me and seemed to relax. For the first time since I'd seen her standing on the porch, she looked happy.

"You like snakes too?"

I didn't get a chance to answer her, because right then her

mama appeared out of nowhere. She snatched Eva up by the arm and pulled her towards the house, never saying a word to either one of us. Eva hardly had a chance to get turned around before her mama pushed her through the door. She'd been tugging on her like a rag doll as Eva walked backwards so she could look at me. She hadn't looked at me at all until scarcely a minute before, and then she wouldn't stop.

"It was nice meeting you," I said from my spot at the spring-house to the back door as it closed. I'd wanted to run after Eva, and ask her to come back to visit, but had stayed right where I was, not wanting to get any closer to her mama than I had to.

My parents didn't say much about the Elliotts after dinner. Mama always said, if you can't say anything nice about someone then you shouldn't say anything at all. I guess she was sticking to her guns when it came to Mrs. Elliott.

But I couldn't wait to see Eva again. I wanted to ask her what she meant about me liking snakes. I also wanted to ask her what to expect at the revival and to invite her to sit with us, but she was nowhere to be found. I looked for her at the corner where her parents held their sidewalk sermons but couldn't find her anywhere. It was like she didn't exist.

\* \* \*

Nothing I'd been told—overheard or imagined—could've prepared me for what happened under the white canvas of the tent that night.

The weather was beautiful, so Mama and Daddy decided

we'd walk to the revival instead of taking Daddy's car. We could hear the music playing from a quarter of a mile away. Tambourines and guitars competed to be heard over the loud voices singing a hymn I didn't recognize.

As we got closer I realized it was one that we sang every Sunday, but it sounded different coming through the canvas walls of the tent. We just had Mrs. Shelton playing the piano at our church while people stood and sang—not yelled—from their hymnbooks.

When we pulled back the slit in the wall to enter, the stench of sweat and the noise from the speakers was enough to almost knock me down. I grabbed ahold of my brother's arm and put my hand up to my nose to keep from breathing in the smell of body odor, hair grease, and talcum powder. Mama saw me out of the corner of her eye and gave me a shake of her head. She was always reminding me that I was a young lady. Apparently young ladies didn't stand holding their noses at a church service, even one held inside a tent. I dropped my hand and took small shallow breaths through my mouth instead.

"Oh, my…" Mama let slip as we took in the chaos at the pulpit. There was Mrs. Elliott, dancing to the music with her hands held high, her big, boxy hips swaying under her ugly brown dress. Her Pentecostal bun—as I'd heard Mama refer to it from my hiding place under the stairs—had come undone and her coarse, gray hair was covering most of her face, hanging down to her waist in tangles.

She didn't seem to notice that her hair had come loose or anything else for that matter. Sweat ran down her face as she danced and yelled over the speakers. I was surprised to see so many people I didn't recognize since I knew everybody who lived in our town. Most of the people were strangers, and they had to have come from other places. I thought to myself it was no wonder they hadn't wanted to use or church for their revival; half of the people wouldn't have fit inside.

My parents tried to lead us to the back, but people stood in the aisles—some dancing, some holding their arms up over their heads—blocking the way. They finally decided to sit where we were, in the section on the right of the pulpit only two rows from the front row.

Mama took Daddy's hand and Hank made a face at me that would've made me laugh if I hadn't been so wound up. Between all the smells and the noise my senses were on overdrive.

I was glad we had to sit in the second row, because I could study the dancing Mrs. Elliott all I wanted. She was nothing like the stern woman who'd sat at our table like a statue.

I was finally able to tear my eyes away from the way Mrs. Elliott's hair swung from her head like some kind of animal hanging on for dear life when I saw her wipe the sweat from her face and sling it onto the person standing next to her.

I found Eva sitting in the front row to our left. I could see her profile staring straight ahead. She was so little that I'd looked right over her at first glance, but her hair caught my eye. It was pulled up in a bun, smaller than a cathead biscuit, on the back of her head the same as it'd been the first time I saw her. And like before, it looked like it was tight enough to hurt. I could see her scalp in places all the way from where I sat. I felt bad for whining about Mama putting a bow in my hair. I'd said it hurt, when actually, I'd forgotten that it was even there.

Eva's father was nowhere to be found, but then the music stopped and I expected him to come in through the same opening we had. The women and men who were dancing in the area between the stage and the first row of seats stopped and turned to face our way.

At first I thought they were staring at us and I almost peed myself, but I quickly realized that they were looking past us, toward the back of the tent. After shaking off the willies, I turned too, and saw what had their attention. The Reverend had appeared through a hidden place in the back and he was holding a big wooden crate. I turned back in my seat to see if I could catch Eva's attention, but she was still facing straight ahead.

Her father yelled out in the same voice he used on the corner, and his voice carried over our heads. *"And these here signs shall follow them that be-lieve; in my name shall they cast out dev-ils; they shall speak with new tongues. They shall take up ser-pents; and if they drink any dead-ly thang, it shall not hurt them; they shall lay hands on the s-ick, and they shall re-cover!!"*

My ears perked up at the mention of serpents and poison. I forgot about Eva and focused on her daddy instead.

He made his way up the aisle, his face red and sweaty, the muscles straining in his neck. I wasn't sure if it was from the weight of the crate or if he looked like that because he was yelling so loud, but he looked like he was about to have a heart attack.

Hallelujahs, brothers and amens were shouted from all over.

*"Be-hold, I give un-to you power to tread on ser-pents and*

*scorp-i-ons, and over all the power of the enemy, and nothing shall by any means hurt you!!"*

"Hallelujah!" Someone yelled in the same row we were sitting in and I almost yelped.

Reverend Elliot, put down the crate on the small stage and picked up a bible from the pulpit. He didn't open it but raised it over his head like he did during his sidewalk sermons.

*"Are you a warrior for Christ? Are you, children?! Are you pre- pared to wage war-fare against the devil?!"*

He was pointing at people, hollering and shaking his head like he was disgusted with everyone he saw. The people he pointed at either nodded and yelled back in agreement or cried and covered their faces in shame.

*"I see a room f-ull of sinners, let me tell you!! I see you women, faces paint-ed, beads a dang-lin' from your earlobes and twisted 'round your necks—just askin' for the devil to come into your homes!! You men, with whiskey on your breath and tobacco in your cheeks —it's a shame, the way you carry on!!"*

He glared down at everyone, using the bible in his hand to point out people he thought were the worst sinners of the bunch. I watched, shocked, as quite a few got up and walked to the front of the church, shouting for forgiveness and yelling hallelujah. I was waiting for someone to take offense, half expecting an argument to start up, but no one challenged the man with the bible. They all looked like scolded hounds or half whipped mules trying to please their owners.

Out of nowhere a man appeared at the end of our row and handed Daddy a basket full of crumpled bills. Daddy added some money and passed it down and I realized that the man was collecting tithes. In all the years of putting money into the offering plate at our church, I'd never even thought about how much money was actually collected. I noticed several other men with similar baskets being passed around and thought about what Hank had said. For the first time in my life, I wondered what happened to tithes that were collected in church.

*"Faith without sacrifice is not faith at all!! Let us pray..."*

I wasn't about to close my eyes. I looked around at everyone with their heads bowed and wondered if they really believed him. Did they really believe that they were such horrible people?

I turned towards Eva and was startled to see her staring straight at her daddy. He had his face raised to the ceiling of the tent and his eyes were closed so he couldn't see her, but still, the defiance in her thin, pale profile surprised me. I twisted in my seat and studied all the people around us. Even my parents and my brother had their heads bowed. Eva and I seemed to be the only ones not obeying.

The only ones with our eyes open.

I jumped when the prayer was over and everyone shouted, "AMEN!!"

The music started again, and things got even crazier than before. That's when the Reverend Elliott opened the crate.

I could see his hands shaking, could almost feel the vibrations from them reaching out to the second row as he unhooked the single latch that held the top in place.

*"We ain't worshippin' a picture of some long-haired man. No sir!"* The sweat shone on his face as he shouted, *"He's a liv-*

*ing God ... God ain't up in the sky somewheres, floatin' around on some white cloud, preenin' his wings. He's a livin' God!"*

He hopped around as he yelled, from one foot to the other and then straight up on the toes of both feet. It looked like he was playing a silly game of charades and I wanted to make a joke at how silly he looked. I leaned towards Hank, but he was staring wide-eyed at the stage. I spun around just in time to see Reverend Elliott as he reached into the crate and pulled out not one but three of the ugliest, fattest copperheads I'd ever seen. They coiled around his arm, one looking him right in the eye. Mama gasped and squeezed my hand hard. I didn't pull away, even though it hurt.

*"Now, He's a spirit. He's a real, true spirit. He ain't got no body, but He's alive just the same! He ain't got a body of his own, the only body He's got is us... And when we're borned again, we're borned into the body of God!"*

This got more amens and hallelujahs and a couple of people fell out on the floor. No lie, they fell onto the beaten down grass and rolled around like they were in pain or having some kind of fit. Mrs. Elliott was speaking in a language I'd never heard before. She was sweating and crying and dancing around again with her hands over her head. She looked plumb ridiculous if you asked me. I looked at Eva to see if she was embarrassed by her parents, but she didn't seem to notice anything or anyone.

*"The disciple Paul did not suffer any effects of a poisonous viper bite! God changed Moses' rod into a serpent and he just picked it up by the tail, children!. PICKED IT UP BY THE TAIL! When the spirit of the Lord is on you, you are not afraid of them*

*serpents! You must believe that the Lord is looking out for you. If you are pure, if you are a warrior, they won't getcha!"*

With that he reached in with his other hand and picked up two more snakes. I'm not sure but I thought I heard a rattle coming from one of them. Rattlers and copperheads. No doubt about it, he was crazy as a loon.

Mama whispered something in Daddy's ear, and I saw him nod. They started sliding to the aisle and she let go of my hand to steady herself. We had a clear path now that everyone who had been standing in the aisles had made it down to the space between the first row and the pulpit. Hank was already at the opening and I could feel the fresh air rush in beside him.

I'd turned for one last look at Eva even though Hank was shaking his head and motioning for me to hurry. I located her just in time to see her mother slap her hard across the face.

I froze. The God we'd been taught to believe in was a loving, caring God, a forgiving God. I don't think he cared one bit if my mama pinned a cameo to her dress or cut her hair, but I do think he would be upset by the slapping and hitting going on up front. That didn't seem very Christian to me.

Hank grabbed me by my arm and pulled me out of the tent, "Dangit, Sister. This ain't the time to be lollygagging. Ain't you seen enough?"

I couldn't answer. For once I couldn't talk at all. Hank held onto my arm until we were halfway home and I was glad he did.

Nobody said anything on the walk home, and Hank and I went straight to bed without any fuss. I guess we were all in a sort of shock.

* * *

As crazy as it seemed, some of the old timers enjoyed the service on Wednesday and asked the Elliotts to stay on for a while. Mr. Carnton told them they could stay in his in-law's cabin if they wanted to and they moved in within hours.

I was torn when I heard the news. Part of me wanted them to go away. The Reverend and his wife gave me such a bad feeling that I wanted them to leave so I could forget about them and what I'd seen. But on the other hand, I wanted them to stay, because I thought that meant Eva would go to school. I wanted someone new to talk to, especially someone who could answer my questions. I didn't realize it then, but what I really wanted was a friend.

When my parents heard the news they had some neighbors over for coffee and invited Brother Talley. He assured everybody that he was still going to have our Sunday service and that there was nothing to worry about. He said he thought that the Elliotts were sent to us for a reason.

"Maybe it's good to get shaken up a bit." He took his time looking around the table, "Maybe it's good to have our faith tested."

* * *

When Monday morning came I searched for Eva at school, but she wasn't in the classroom.

When it was time to break for lunch, I hurried to get my pail and ran outside to sit in my favorite spot before anyone else could get it. It wasn't that I didn't like the other kids in my class, but Rodney and his friends were bullies, and the girls my age talked about boring stuff. Mostly they talked about how cute they thought Rodney was. He wasn't. And Hank was too busy trying to get Kati's attention to give any to me.

I'd just sat down when I saw something move in the bushes out of the corner of my eye. I turned my head quickly and saw a bright flash of orange before it was hidden behind the trunk of a maple tree.

I put down my lunch and tiptoed over to the edge of the schoolyard. I crouched in the weeds, steady as a level, and waited until Eva peeked out from her hiding place. As soon as she saw me I jumped up and smiled.

"Hi, Eva," I laughed, "I thought you were a fox."

We stood there staring at each other, until I saw some of the older kids going towards my seat. I motioned for her to follow me and ran back to claim it. She surprised me by coming and sat down beside me on the huge root of an ancient oak that was shaped like a bench. I gave her half of my sandwich without asking if she wanted it and started talking.

I told her everything I knew about our teacher. Mrs. Dorris had three dogs, two cats, one yellow bird that she said was a canary, and no husband.

"She's pretty nice, as long as you don't act up. Sometimes

she brings her bird to class and hangs his cage on a hook by the window." I thought Eva would like that, but she didn't even smile.

"Are you going to start class tomorrow?" I asked.

"No."

"But…why not?" I asked.

"I ain't allowed."

"Not allowed?" I'd never heard of anyone not being allowed to go to school.

Eva shook her head and placed the sandwich on her lap. With her right hand, she took off the top piece of bread, and smelled the salty goodness of the slice of ham underneath. I'd always wanted to do that too, but Mama wouldn't have liked it. I was about to tell her that when she took a huge bite. The way she ate reminded me of the barn cats that showed up out of nowhere. She ate fast, like she was scared someone was going to take her food away, and for a second I thought she might choke.

When she finished, I gave her the other half of my sandwich and one of my teacakes, hoping she would use both hands to hold them. But she kept the left hand wrapped up in her skirt. I forgot all of the questions I wanted to ask her and focused on that instead. There had to be some reason she kept it hidden.

Maybe she had a little hand. I knew someone else who had a little hand. He used to work at the grocery. He had one hand that was normal for his size and one hand that looked like a baby's. I didn't know why it was like that. I always wanted to ask him, but Mama would've tanned my hide for being rude. He didn't try to hide it, though, and if he saw you staring, he'd touch the tip of your nose with it.

No matter how many times Mama threatened me before we went in the store not to stare, I always got touched on the nose. I couldn't help it and he seemed to think it was funny that I tilted my face up to him instead of turning away. He'd grin and I would giggle. He wasn't embarrassed at all. I liked him and cried when I heard he was moving to Kentucky to live with his brother. I cried so hard the last time I saw him, that I missed my chance to ask him about his hand and I don't even remember if he touched my nose goodbye.

I was trying to think about how to tell her about the man who worked at the general store so she wouldn't be worried about it. After all, I'd seen one before. But when I opened my mouth to tell her, Rodney Lassiter ran by with a bunch of boys that were always causing trouble.

"Hey, Delene, catch!" he yelled and threw a frog at us. Startled, Eva put up both hands to shield her face from the flying green missile. It landed on her head and I got a look at her left hand.

"Here, let me help. The poor thing's terrified." I said and stood up, partly to hide the look on my face from Eva.

Eva's hand was covered with scars and it looked like her little finger was stuck to the one beside it. All four fingers were bent and looked like they couldn't be straightened.

Somehow he burrowed himself in her bun and as we worked on getting the frog loose, her sleeve slid down and I could see more scars on the white skin of her wrist and part of her arm.

Whatever had happened to her had to have hurt like the dickens. It wasn't something she'd been born with after all. Something horrible had happened, and I noticed that her right hand was scarred too, but not as bad as her left.

When I finally got him to let go, I took the poor frog over to some tall grass behind the school and let him go, far away from Rodney and far enough away that I could calm myself.

When I walked back to the shade of the oak tree, Eva was gone.


I couldn't stop wondering what had happened to her. I looked for her that whole week. But if she'd been hiding in the woods by the schoolyard, I couldn't find her. If anyone else saw her, they never mentioned her to me.

* * *

Not too long after that I was down at our creek by myself, catching crawdads for Daddy to use for fishing bait. I loved it when he and Hank caught a mess of fish and Mama fried them up for dinner. I didn't like fishing myself, I could never sit still long enough to catch anything, but I loved to eat them. Mama fried her crispy hush puppies with green onions in the oil she used to fry the fish and I would eat so many of them I'd almost make myself sick.

I was having a good day, I'd caught a bunch of nice sized crawdads, a salamander with a bright orange belly, and found a perfect arrowhead. I'd been wishing I had someone to show all of my treasures to when I heard something on the other side of the bank. It was Eva walking in the tall grass carrying a burlap sack like the kind Mama Gladys used at her store to hold rice or potatoes. I was thinking about what to say, trying hard to keep from splashing through the water and chasing her off when she dropped the sack and knelt down. I could barely see the top of her head over the weeds.

"Hey Eva!" I yelled when I couldn't stand it any longer.

I didn't think she'd heard me, but then she stood up.

"He's beautiful, ain't he?" she asked, and held up a snake by its tail for me to see. I didn't answer, but she didn't seem to mind.

"What are you doin' all the way out here?" she asked as she opened the sack and let the snake slither inside.

I stopped staring at the sack and looked at her instead. I'd never heard her say more than one or two words at a time and her voice sounded different than I remembered.

"Our place comes to the side of the creek." I said, pointing in the direction of our house.

"We're stayin' in a cabin up that way."

"Yeah, old man Hibbert's place butts up against ours." I said, hoping to keep the conversation going but after a minute of silence I thought Eva was going to leave without saying anything else.

But she surprised me. Eva looked over the edge of the creekbank.

"What're you doin' down there?"

"Catching crawdads. Want to help?" I smiled up at her.

"I ain't never caught one before." She answered, sounding

40

doubtful.

I pointed at the burlap sack and said, "If you can catch snakes, you can catch crawdads no problem."

Eva grinned and made her way down the bank. I waited until she set the sack down and then tied her skirt up between her legs and around her waist. I worked fast before she had time to protest, then went right on to show her where to look for crawdads under the rocks. She tried catching them with only her right hand, but I told her she'd have to use them both.

"One hand in front of the crawdad and the other behind him to scoop him up."

She quit smiling.

"I already saw your hand anyway. You don't have to hide it from me." I acted like I couldn't care less about it, even though I wanted to look at it up close more than anything else I could think of. I wanted to touch her skin and see what it felt like. I wanted to know how far up the scars went. I wanted to ask her what happened. I wanted to know if it still hurt. But I went on about my business catching crawdads and kept my mouth shut.

Soon she was catching them too. We were having so much fun I'd almost forgotten about her hand until Eva caught a big blue crawdad that pinched her and wouldn't let go.

"Ouch!" she yelped, shaking her hand which caused him to hold on tighter.

I took her hand and held it in my left hand while I pulled the pincher off with my right one.

Before I could stop myself, I rubbed her knuckles with my thumb. They felt like leather. I looked up at her and she was staring at me and I felt the same way as I had the first time she looked at me. That same electric current shot through me and circled back to Eva. I smiled and let go of her hand.

"What are you catching all those snakes for?"

Eva seemed to have forgotten all about them. She turned towards the sack and shrugged.

"Are those for your daddy?"

"Naw, those are for me."

I opened my mouth to ask what for, but Eva cut me off.

"It ain't right to keep them in those crates so long, but he don't care one thing about them. I'm the one that takes care of them. I catch them field mice and lizards to eat and make sure they have water and stuff. After a while, I let them go and find new ones. He's too scared to catch them himself."

I narrowed my eyes at her, sure she was teasing me, but she wasn't. She was scowling.

"Eva, we came to the revival that first night. If he's scared of snakes, then how could he hold them and carry on like he does?" I asked. Then, before I could stop myself, I put my hands up over my head and danced around with a goofy look on my face, mimicking her daddy.

She looked shocked, and then bent over laughing.

"I'll tell you a secret, but you have to promise not to tell nobody." Eva said.

"I promise." I said before she even finished the sentence. I loved secrets more than I loved asking questions.

"I milk the snakes so they don't have poison in them before Daddy will touch them." Eva grinned at me and I noticed she had

42

a tiny scar on her cheek that looked like a dimple.

I thought of how her daddy's hands shook when he reached inside of the crate at the revival.

"Oh yeah, even without the poison he's scared of their teeth. He has to drink corn liquor before each sermon so he has the nerve to hold them." She quit grinning and looked at me.

"He'd beat me senseless if he knew I told anybody."

"I promise I won't tell." I said and blurted out the first question of many.

"But...milk a snake? I didn't even know they had udders."

"It ain't like that!" Eva bent over laughing and I couldn't help but laugh too. When she finished, she told me that milking a snake meant taking out its poison. She explained how she did it in the same way Mama had explained how to make a skillet of cornbread or beat a bowl of egg whites until they peaked. Like it was the most natural thing in the world.

"Want me to show you?" Eva asked, pointing towards the sack.

"No thanks," I answered quickly and changed the subject.

"So, how does your daddy keep from getting blistered when he handles fire?"

She laughed. "I ain't never seen him touch a single flame, that's how he keeps from getting blistered."

"Are you saying..."

"That he tells tall tales?" Eva asked then reached down to snatch up a crawdad that backed into her foot.

"Have you ever told anybody?" I asked.

She held up the crawdad for me to see, her eyes as bright

43

green as new clover. She dropped it in the bucket, then looked back at me.

"I never had no one to tell it to. Nobody's ever asked me any questions before."

"Well you do now, I have a bunch of questions and I want to hear everything." I said.

Standing in water up to our ankles, Eva emptied a lifetime of words right there at the creek.

"I like the cabin. I've got a room in the loft all to myself. It has a palette I don't have to share, and I found a wren's nest in the corner with eggs in it. It's got a real window that I can close, but I keep it open for the mama bird to get in and out whenever she wants. But the best part is that Mama can't fit through the narrow openin' to come up there, and Daddy can't make it up the rickety ladder after he's been drinkin'," she reached down to turn over a rock, "so they leave me alone at night."

I had no idea what she meant by that, and almost asked, but I bit my tongue and let her talk.

"I hate movin' around all the time."

"You never had a house of your own before?" I asked.

"We used to, but that was a long time ago. Before Matthew died."

"Who was Matthew?" I asked as I put another crawdad in the bucket.

"He was my brother, but he died a long time ago."

"Oh," I stopped looking for crawdads and looked at her, "I'm sorry."

"Me too." She said and walked a few steps away to turn over another rock.

She'd quit talking, but I had more questions. I wasn't sure if she wanted to talk about him anymore or not, then I remembered what she said about no one asking her anything, so I asked.

"What was he like?"

"He looked just like Daddy and he wanted to be a preacher too. But not like daddy's kind of preachin'. He was fun, always laughin' and cuttin' up. He used to take me for piggyback rides and make up funny stories. He told me my hair meant I was good luck, and he always wanted me near." Eva stopped and looked down the creek like she was looking for her brother. When she turned to me I saw a flash behind her golden lashes.

"I'm goin' to tell you another secret. You really promise you won't tell nobody?" she asked. I was already nodding before she finished the question, eager to hear whatever she was going to tell me.

"Daddy cain't read. Matthew had been teachin' him how. He used to read to him from the Bible and help Daddy prepare his sermons. Now that Matthew is gone, he just repeats the same old ones over and over. The ones that Matthew was tryin' to get him to change."

"Oh." I remembered how Reverend Elliott waved the bible around and never opened it.

"They blame me for his death. And I reckon they're right. After all, I asked him to hold up Mr. Lester."

"Mr. Lester?" I asked.

She took hold of my wrist to make sure I was paying attention. "Delene, Daddy used to have boys bring snakes to the house and he'd trade them for moonshine. One day they showed up with a trough in the back of their truck with a piece of metal on top, sayin' they had Mr. Lester."

"They had somebody in there?" I couldn't believe my ears.

"Naw. Not somebody. It was a snake named after Mr. Lester. He was a mean old man who'd shoot your dog if he crossed his yard. Mean as the devil. Everybody was afraid of him. So Daddy asked them to show him what they had but wouldn't nobody get near enough to lift the metal lid. I begged Matthew to hold me up on his shoulder so I could see, then I kept on until he slid off the lid. That snake was mad. Delene, his rattles sounded like a motor hummin'. He was skint up, too. Those boys had roughed him up somethin' awful."

I felt her hand squeeze my wrist.

"I never should've asked him to do it, I never should've said nothin', but those boys were callin' Matthew a sissy. Teasin' him and actin' foolish."

She took a deep breath and sighed.

"Why did I have to get him killed?"

"It wasn't your fault, Eva. It was that dang snake that did it. Not you."

"No, Delene. It was pride that done it."

Eva let go of me and went back to hunting crawdads. I tried, but my heart wasn't in it. I blindly turned over rocks while I thought about everything she'd said. It was a lot more than I'd expected and I was trying to remember it all so I could pick it apart later. I'd never heard anything that compared to Eva's story.

It beat a finger packed on ice any day.


When it was time to for me to go home, Eva pointed at my bucket and asked, "What are you goin' to do with them things anyway?"

"Daddy uses them for fishing bait."

"You reckon he'll need more tomorrow?" She asked.

"Oh, no...these'll last him awhile!" We'd filled the bucket almost full and I couldn't wait to show him. I'd never caught that many before, not even with Hank. I laughed, tickled with myself, but noticed Eva was frowning.

"Oh, I was hopin' we could catch some more tomorrow."

Before I could talk myself out of it, I turned the bucket upside down and let the crawdads loose. As I watched them run backwards for new hiding places, I fought the urge to grab them back. But I wasn't sure Eva would want to meet me without having a reason, or if she would talk like she did without having the crawdads to keep her busy.

"What did you do that for?"

"I guess I'll see you here tomorrow." I said with a shrug and broke out in giggles while Eva stared at me like I'd sprouted a second nose, or another set of ears. I couldn't stop giggling, but Eva never even smiled.

"Alrighty then." She finally answered and we made our way out of the creek.

"Right here, tomorrow?" I called out to Eva.

I held my breath until she nodded. Then we smiled at each

other on the opposite sides of the creek.

Me with my empty bucket, and Eva with a sack full of snakes.

I looked for her in the schoolyard next day, but if she was hiding in the bushes, I couldn't find her. I'd talked myself into a good worry by the time school let out. I convinced myself that she regretted telling me her secrets and I would never see her again. But when I was finally able to get to the creek, she was there waiting.

"You know, you're lucky. Luckier than me and you ain't even got red hair."

I stopped working on her skirt and looked up at her.

"How so?" I asked, thinking she was talking about the fact I had on a pair of Hank's hand me down pants that were rolled up past my knees. If that was the case, I'd bring her a pair the next day.

"I watched your mama for a little while today. I wasn't snooping – she just happened to be outside when I was over that way."

Eva pointed towards the field across from our house.

"Did you know there's a patch of blackberries over yonder? Some of them berries are as big as eggs."

I shook my head. Hank and I were told to stay out of the fields across the road. They were overgrown and likely full of snakes, but I guessed that was a bonus for Eva.

"I watched her hangin' out laundry. She was smilin' and singin' the whole time."

That kind of surprised me and made me think about how much Eva and I had in common. I recalled all the times I'd spied on her mama. I'd never thought someone might think my family was interesting enough to notice, but I guess to Eva we were the ones that were different.

"When I grow up I want to be just like her, but I'm goin' to marry a farmer instead of a banker and live in a house next to a barn full of animals. And I'm goin' to have at least ten kids."

I laughed, "I want to marry a farmer, too, but I don't want ten kids! Lordy, you'd need a wagon to haul them around in."

That made Eva laugh so hard we got tangled up in her skirts and almost fell in the water. The next thing I knew we were splashing each other and laughing like we didn't have a care in the world.

When Eva laughed it was a powerful thing.

After we'd caught a mess of crawdads, I invited Eva to come to my house.

"I cain't. I ain't supposed to leave our property or talk to nobody. I told them I found the blackberries down here, but I didn't tell them about you. They cain't find out or I'd be..."

"Stuck with them on the corner all day?" I pictured Eva marching behind her mama and it made me sad.

"No, I'd be stuck in the cabin. They don't want me down there, they only want me with them on Wednesdays in case Daddy has to prove a miracle. But so far, just seein' daddy handlin'

49

snakes has been enough."

"Prove a miracle?" I had no idea what she was talking about.

"It's just a lot of nonsense." Eva grinned, "These people are bigger suckers than most. I hope we never have to leave."

That night after dinner, Hank came in my room.

"I saw you and that red-haired girl today."

"Were you spying on me?"

"No, I was going fishing and heard y'all laughing. I just watched you for a minute. I swear." Hank held up his hand, "Scout's honor."

"Well, stop it. You might run her off. She's not supposed to be down there and you might scare her away."

"You know that money that was missing? The money for the roof? Well, somebody put it back in Mrs. Howard's desk drawer."

"Really?" I got excited. Nothing ever happened here. "Was it Joel King?"

"Sis, why would you think that?" Hank laughed and shook his head.

"Because he's always buying flowers for Tammy Lynne. Maybe he didn't mean to steal it, only borrow it and put it back before anybody noticed."

Hank rolled his eyes and got serious again.

"No, it wasn't Joel King. Funny thing was when the money came up missing Brother Talley was over in Dozier. He got a ride with one of the Jompson brothers and they ended up staying longer than they expected."

"Well, we knew it wasn't Brother Talley you big dummy." I shook my head.

"Of course we did, but whoever tried to set him up made a mistake and had to fix it." Hank squinted his eyes at me. "Somebody said they saw a little red-haired girl around the church."

"That's the dumbest thing I ever heard. She don't even go into town because her parents don't want her to. She'd get in trouble." I almost yelled, "And anyway. Eva wouldn't steal anything. She's not like that."

"What are y'all doing anyway?"

"Just playing." I had to turn my back to him because I wasn't good at lying. I'd promised not to tell anything about her Daddy, which wasn't that hard because Hank wouldn't care about him not being able to read. At least I didn't think so. But if I slipped up and told him about Eva catching snakes it would be a mess. I knew Hank, he'd want to see for himself. He'd tell Aaron and every other boy he knew, and they'd all come down. Plus, if Mama found out, she wouldn't let me anywhere near Eva's burlap sack. Which meant no more Eva because she never went anywhere without it.

"We talk about girl stuff," I struggled to think of something, "like kissing boys, and having babies. Stuff like that."

"Yuck, Delene." His answer gave me courage. I spun around and took a step towards him.

"Why don't you come down there tomorrow. Maybe you could tell us what kissing is like. I know you and Kati do it."

"You wouldn't catch me anywhere near y'all talking about that stuff. And be quiet, you don't know anything about what me and Kati do."

"Oh yes I do. You keep spying on me and I'll start spying on you." I closed my eyes and puckered up my lips. "Oh, Hank!"

I chased him out of my room making kissing noises and went to bed satisfied. I was pretty sure Hank wouldn't bring up Eva again.

The next afternoon, Eva had managed to tie up her skirt and was already in the water when I got there. I wondered what she did all day while I sat in class. Picking blackberries and catching snakes had to get tiresome. She was bound to get bored being alone all the time.

"Eva, why aren't you allowed to go to school?" I asked.

"Mama says she teaches me everythin' I need to know. I ain't ever been 'cause we move around so much. Matthew used to go, and he taught me my letters and stuff. I still practice sometimes." Eva shrugged.

I was tired of catching the same old crawdads every day. It took a little coaxing to get her to come out of the creek, but I argued that our toes were going to get so wrinkled they'd never straighten out if we stayed in the water all the time.

"We can still talk. We don't have to be catching crawdads to do it. I like listening to you." I said and meant it.

One afternoon, hidden by pine trees and dogwoods that separated our yard from the rest of the property, we chased butterflies in the field behind my house. We came up on a little fawn and I knew it's mama was somewhere close. I took hold of Eva and drew her with me, tiptoeing away from it so we wouldn't scare him off. I realized I had her left hand in mine and she hadn't pulled away. When we were away from the deer, she pressed her hand into my palm, and I felt the same feeling as before. That current of electricity passed through us and into the ground beneath my feet. I rubbed my thumb across her knuckles and hoped I wasn't about to mess up. Eva was my friend and I didn't want to do anything to change that.

"Eva, how'd you get these scars?"

She looked at her hand for a minute without speaking. Then she told me the worst story I'd ever heard in my life. After all these years, I still haven't heard one that compares to hers. What still gets me to this very day is that she told it to me without shedding a single tear.

"Well, I told you I had a brother, remember? I told you it was my fault he died, I was the one who killed him."

"It wasn't your fault, Eva." I said, but she went on.

"It all happened so fast, Delene. I cain't remember everything. Matthew got bit, then Daddy was carryin' him to the house and yellin' at them boys to chop up Mr. Lester with an ax. But I was cryin' and beggin' them not to. It didn't seem right. It wasn't his fault. It was my fault – my pride. Mr. Lester…he was scared and hurt. He was mad, Delene. Matthew wouldn't want them to kill him, he wouldn't hurt a fly. I was holdin' the axe and wouldn't let them boys have it. Daddy come runnin' back out and slapped me hard across the face and yanked the axe out of my hand. I thought he was going to do it himself, but he changed his mind. He told them to put the snake in one of the wooden crates behind our house.

As afraid of Mr. Lester as they were, they were more afraid of my daddy when he was angry. Well, the same night they laid Matthew out, Daddy sat up until mornin' drinkin' whiskey. When I woke up he was standin' in my door starin' at me, then him and mama got to fightin' and he had the first bad spell I remember. Next thing I know, he put me in the crate with Mr. Lester, and closed me up in there. I tried to open the crate, but I couldn't do it. I don't know how many times I got bit and I ain't sure how long I was in there, or who took me out. I just know I got really sick.

Daddy was even worse after that. Instead of thinkin' of the words he preached—the ones about how God will protect you from the serpents if you're pure? If you believe? He thought I was defyin' him. That's what he said, I was defyin' him." Eva shook her head and took a breath.

"It don't make no sense that Matthew died and I didn't. Daddy and Mama thought I was defyin' them and God himself, by livin' when Matthew died so quick. After that they did all kinds of stuff. Burned me, poured lye on me, made me drink lye and kerosene. No matter what, I…I don't know why not… but I didn't die."

"After a while they figured out how to use me to make money. All them other places we came from, people would fill the baskets to see a miracle. But they got in trouble and we had to leave. We've been movin' around ever since." Eva snorted.

"Ain't no such things as miracles. They know it, same as me. That's why they hate me, they think I'm mockin' them. That's why daddy goes through his bad spells and why I make myself invisible."

"Oh, Eva. That's awful." I hadn't realized I was crying until I tasted the salt from the tears on my lips.

"Yeah, but Delene, there's a whole lot of awful stuff out there. I ain't the only one it happens to, you should see some of the people that are brung to my daddy for a healin'. I know I'll die just like everybody else one day, there ain't nothin' special about me." Eva pulled away and gave me a playful shove, "I ain't a miracle by no means, I'm just hardheaded I reckon."

I tried to think of the worst thing that had happened to me and the only thing I could think of was the time Rodney stuck a piece of licorice in my hair.

"Where is your mama when your daddy's doing those things to you, when he's having a bad spell?" I asked her.

What she said caused my heart to skip a beat. She said her mama is always there beside her father, dancing and shouting and speaking in tongues.

Eva said, "I think it's my mama who brings on daddy's bad spells."


\* \* \*


The next day I had two questions for Eva. I'd not slept a wink the night before, thinking about what she told me. Every time I closed my eyes, I kept picturing her – closed up in that crate.

"How can you catch snakes like you do? Ain't you scared to death, especially after what happened?"

Eva put her hands on her bony hips and shrugged her shoulders.

"I cain't explain it. I know it sounds crazy, but until you – snakes were the only friends I ever had."

For two whole weeks, as soon as I was out of school, and after we'd done our chores, we'd meet at the creek and play. Eva let me hold her hand without thinking twice now, no longer self-conscious of her scars. We'd hold hands and run up and down the muddy bank like wild ponies.

We'd stopped catching crawdads and I'd started braiding Eva's hair. When it was braided, it looked like it was mixed with golden thread. The same golden thread that made her eyelashes sparkle like tiny diamonds had been woven in between each lash. Especially when the sun hit it.

She'd never had anyone braid her hair before and would stare at her reflection in the water like she couldn't believe it was her looking back.

"Mama would skin me alive if she saw me looking at myself like this."

"Well, she's not here, so look all you want." I teased her, but I liked sitting beside her and looking at our reflections in the water as much as she did. I thought we looked like sisters.

We always made sure to put her hair back in the same little knot before Eva went home. Every hair pulled back tight enough I was afraid it hurt, but Eva never complained.

Sometimes we'd pretend we were married women and have dinner parties with our make-believe husbands. We'd pick wild-flowers for our centerpieces and use bark for our dishes. Our fine dining table was an old stump in the back of our field. I'd bring tea cakes or biscuits with molasses and whipped butter, whatever treat Mama had for me and Henry, and watch Eva savor every crumb. She said she'd never tasted anything so good and I thought of all the times I'd eaten them without giving them a second thought.

I'd never considered myself lucky, I mean I knew Mama was good, but I'd taken her for granted. Before I met Eva, I'd assumed that every mama made sweets for their children and tucked them in at night. I thought every daddy went to work and came home happy with stories to tell at the dinner table, and a kiss on the cheek before bedtime.

Eva had none of those things, and she didn't hold a single grudge against me for having all that and more.

We never brought up anything from her past. It's hard to explain, but once Eva put down the burden of all those stories and secrets, they just didn't seem to be a part of her.

We played like normal kids every afternoon and I'd gotten so used to our schedule at the creek, I'd convinced myself everything was going to be like that forever. That Eva's life had changed and before long, she'd be coming to my house for a sleepover.

But of course that didn't happen. About two weeks later, Eva told me that she wouldn't be able to meet me every day. The people coming to the revival were getting bored with the snakes and her parents were getting anxious.

We still met whenever we could, but Eva wasn't as talkative as she'd been before. We didn't run and laugh as much. Actually, we didn't play at all.

A lot of the time, those last few days, Eva was busy catching snakes.

I'd trail along at a safe distance and tell her stories while she tracked down water moccasins sunning on flat rocks at the water's edge. I'd watch her, amazed and terrified in equal amounts. She never used a stick or anything to pin them down, she didn't pinch them behind the jaw or grip their necks. Instead, Eva picked them up gently by the tail and held them up high so she could look them in the eyes. I swear, the snakes would stop wiggling when their eyes met, and Eva would give them a little smile before she placed them in her sack. It was like they wanted to get caught.

I assumed that she was catching them for the revival, which was something I didn't want to think about. If the people were bored with her daddy handling snakes, that meant they would be looking for something else more exciting. I knew that meant Eva, and I was afraid that talking about it would bring it on sooner. I wanted us to ignore it as long as we could.

Eva loved hearing how Mama baked short bread and curled her hair. How she would wake me and Hank up with a kiss on our ear and a tickle under our chin. How she would read funny stories to us from books that my grandmother had read to her. I told her how my parents would dance in the kitchen when they thought we were in bed and how Hank and I would watch from the stairs. How Daddy would spin Mama around and make her throw her head back so he could kiss her neck.

That was her favorite part.

I talked Eva into taking a break and letting me braid her hair, which she hadn't let me do in a long time, while I told her the story again.

"He spins her out away from him, then pulls her back so quick her feet come off the ground. Then he dips her back and kisses her all the way up to her chin." I reached around and tickled Eva's neck. I'd missed her laugh and was glad when I got one.

"I changed my mind. I ain't goin' to marry a farmer, I'm goin' to marry someone just like your daddy. Someone who'll dance me around the kitchen like that."

"Well, maybe you'll find yourself a dancing farmer and that way you can still have your barn full of animals." I said and sat down beside her.

We were sitting on the creek bank that warm afternoon, laughing and making plans for Eva's future, when everything changed.


"Eeeeva!" Mrs. Elliott's deep voice thundered across the field, sounding more animal than human.

Eva jumped up and brushed the leaves off her skirt.

"Oh, no. They're home early."

"Don't go home, Eva. Come to my house instead." I stood,

59

but stayed crouched down, afraid Mrs. Elliott would see me and come charging across the field. Just like a bull.

I reached for Eva's hand, but she pulled away before I could get a firm grip around it.

"I cain't."

"Please, please, please come with me. Mama will make us tea cakes and ..." I begged her but she cut me off.

"Your mama cain't protect me from them," she said, her voice suddenly strong. "Cain't nobody help me, Delene, I got to save myself."

Eva reached for the burlap sack and I thought she was going to take off running, but she turned back to me instead, "Delene, you showed me that life is more than just livin' in fear. You and me are friends and I won't never forget you."

"I'll see you tomorrow, right here. Okay?" I begged Eva. "Okay? Promise me."

"Eeeeva!" Mrs. Elliott bellowed again, making her daughter's name sound like a threat.

With a rush of emotion that was so unlike the girl I knew, Eva grabbed my face and kissed my cheek. I took hold of her and hugged her as tight as I could. She let me, but didn't hug me back. Instead she gently pushed me away, picked up the burlap sack and climbed up the bank.

I touched the spot where she'd just kissed me, and it felt hot under my hand. I had a vision of Eva's kiss leaving a scar on my cheek to match the hundreds of scars she carried on her body.

Eva looked back over her shoulder once and waved. I waved back at her and she turned to run the rest of the way across the field. I put my hand over my mouth to keep from screaming Eva's name.

The long, red braid I'd tied with my satin turquoise ribbon sparked and swung between Eva's skinny shoulder blades as she ran towards her mama's voice.

What had I done?

I ran home and burst through the kitchen door straight to Mama. Between sobs, I told Mama that Eva was in trouble. I knew as soon as I started talking, that I should've told her sooner.

Mama tried to stay calm as I cried at the kitchen table.

"We've got to do something, Mama. Right now!" I squalled. But she kept wiping my face with a cool washcloth and I felt worse every time her soft hands touched me. I could only imagine what was happening to Eva.

Mama said that when Daddy came home she'd tell him everything and they would pay the Elliotts a visit. Somehow she managed to get me to change into my gown and talked me into lying down.

But right before I pulled back the covers on my soft warm bed, the courier came with a note saying Daddy had to work late.

"Mama, please call him and tell him he has to come home right now." I pleaded.

"Honey, I can't do that. Our phone is out of order." She held the note up from the courier as proof. "I promise I'll talk to him as soon as he comes in."

"Where's Hank? We can..." I looked out the window, shocked to see it was dark out already. I must've been crying for over an hour.

"Hank's next door helping Mr. Winters. He'll be home later. Right now, you need to do as I say and go to bed, okay? I need a minute to gather my thoughts. We can't go running over there all willy nilly, Delene. We have to have a plan."

I knew Mama had a hard time following everything I'd told her. She hadn't seen the scars or heard the way Mrs. Elliott's voice sounded as she called Eva in. She hadn't felt or seen how scared Eva was.

And I hadn't said a single thing about any of it all this time. Mama hadn't even known I was meeting Eva. I couldn't wait for Daddy to check on Eva. I was afraid of what was happening right now.

I kissed Mama goodnight, went to my room, and shut the door behind me. This was all my fault. I should've told somebody what had happened to Eva sooner.

I went straight to the window and crawled out into the darkness. I went running across the field with my hair flying behind me and my nightgown sticking to my legs, stopping just long enough to grab a lantern from the wellhouse to light the way. If anyone would've seen me they would've thought I was a haint.

* * *

When I got to Eva's cabin, I could see shadows through the windows. I could hear her Daddy's voice loud and clear, like he was preaching a sermon to a room full of people. I put the lantern down and peeked in the nearest window, my heart pounding in my chest. I expected to see some of the people from the revival worshipping Reverend Elliott as he waved his bible over them, but there was only Eva. Standing in the middle of the room, wearing a cotton gown, with her hair loose and hanging over her shoulders. I could see the waves the braid left in her hair, and I could see her bony frame through the thin material of her gown.

I raised my hand to knock on the glass to get Eva's attention just as Mrs. Elliott stepped out of the shadows. I bit my lower lip to keep from crying out as she raised her husband's belt and brought it down across Eva's skinny back. Two solid swings in a row. She hit her daughter hard enough to knock her down, but Eva didn't make a sound.

Mrs. Elliott pulled Eva up by her hair and yanked her back to the center of the room. Then she turned to put the belt on a small table and picked up a candle. I felt a lump form in my throat as the light from the candle picked up the sheen of my satin ribbon stretched out across the table's surface.

She snatched up Eva's arm and raised it until it was horizontal with the floor and yelled at Eva to raise the other one the same way. "Don't act like you don't know what to do, you disrespectful little tramp! Put that arm up or so help me you'll wish you didn't have an arm to raise."

She yelled the last sentence right into Eva's ear, her nose smashed into her daughter's temple. I flinched, but Eva didn't. She raised her arms like she was told.

Mrs. Elliot held the candle flame to the underside of her daughter's thin white arm. My bladder let go, and I felt a warm trickle of water run down my legs when Eva's daddy stepped up beside his wife.

"*With cleansing purifying flame descend on us today! The night is far spent, let us therefore cast off the works of darkness, and let us put on the armor of light take heed to yourselves!!*"

Eva stood as still as a scarecrow. She had the same look on her face that she'd had that Wednesday night inside of the tent, when her mama was dancing and her daddy was yelling, the look on her face when her mama slapped her. She was staring up into the far corner of the room. I knew what she was doing, I remembered what she'd said. She was trying to make herself invisible.

I willed her to look at me, but she didn't seem to be there. For one second it seemed like she *was* disappearing. I blinked and Eva was just an outline of a girl. I had to do something now, before she disappeared forever.

I remembered seeing a pile of field rocks by the well when I'd come running past. I went to get one, fumbling in the dark and almost screamed when my hand closed around something soft. I jerked my hand back and my eyes adjusted to the pale moonlight just in time to see a snake slither away.

I took a deep breath and forced myself to be brave. I reached back down for two good sized rocks and ran back to the house with one in each hand. When I got close enough I drew back and threw the first rock towards the window as hard as I could. Glass shattered and I heard the Reverend and Mrs. Elliott yell out in surprise. Someone ran to the door and threw it open, yelling a threat I couldn't make out from the front porch. I threw the second rock even harder towards the voice and heard a thud, followed by Mrs. Elliott's voice screaming obscenities towards me.

I saw the outline of Mr. Elliot raise a shotgun to his shoulder and heard Mrs. Elliot order her husband to kill me dead.

I panicked and took off running towards home in complete darkness, my lantern left behind. I fell twice crossing the creek but once I made it over the bank, the lights from our house kept me from getting caught up in the briers and stickweed. I heard Daddy's voice and ran harder towards the light.

I burst through the back door, dripping creek water and blood from a cut on my knee onto our clean floor, and ran straight for my Daddy's arms.

"What in the world!" Mama said as her coffee cup fell from her hand. I told them what was happening to Eva and what I'd done. I was surprised when Daddy didn't ask any questions or tell me to calm myself. He was already out the door when Hank came running out of his room.

"Daddy, I'm coming with you." Hank looked at me, "Don't worry little sister, we'll bring your friend back with us."

While we waited for them to come back with Eva, Mama told me that Hank sat her and Daddy down and validated everything I'd told her earlier.

"Honey, he heard me telling Daddy what you'd told me and he got real upset. He's been keeping a close eye on you and Eva. He said he should've done something sooner, but...," she started crying. "I can't believe you went over there all alone, you must've been so scared. I can't believe all of this was happening right under my nose – all these horrible things, and I had no idea."

"I'm sorry I was sneaky Mama. I just wanted to play with Eva, I was afraid you wouldn't let me if you knew..."

She hugged me tight. "None of this is your fault, Delene. I'm sorry I wasn't paying better attention, honey. If I'd been a better listener, you and your brother could've told me sooner."

I was starting to feel like everything was going to be okay, but they came back without her.

.

Daddy and Hank said when they got there, the cabin was dark except for a light in the upstairs window.

"When they finally came to the door, they acted as if they'd been woken from a deep sleep." Daddy shook his head and poured himself a glass of whiskey.

"They acted like they were still half asleep until I asked to see Eva. Her mama went from mumbling to yelling and accused me of all kinds of ..." Daddy looked at me and back at Mama, "things."

"But Daddy wouldn't stop and started yelling for Eva to come down. I ran to the side of the house and tried to get her to come to the window, but she wouldn't. I called her and called her, but it didn't do any good. I could see her shadow up there, moving around. I thought maybe she was getting some things together and she was coming down, but Mrs. Elliott started yelling for her husband to get his gun."

"Did he?" Mama turned to Daddy.

Daddy finished his whiskey and poured another drink.

"Not fast enough for Mrs. Elliott. That crazy old thing went and got it! She ran out with it and almost blew his head off." Hank was full of adrenaline and bouncing in his chair. Mama put her hand on his knee to stop him. "If she hadn't tripped over her two big feet, she would've, Mama. But instead she blew a hole in their porch."

Hank looked at me and managed a grin, "I did see a good-sized knot on Mrs. Elliott's forehead though. Good shot Delene."

I wasn't able to smile back at him. All I could think about was Eva.

"What are you going to do now?" Mama had run to Daddy and had her face buried in his chest. "You can't go back."

"Oh, I'm going back. But I'm going to wait until daylight and I'm not going alone."

Turns out Eva and I weren't the only ones Hank had been keeping an eye on. He and Aaron had been spying on everybody and figured out who the Elliotts got to steal the money to try to get Brother Talley in trouble. It was one of the men that hung around the revival. Instead of being over at Mr. Winter's house Hank had been with Brother Talley at the sheriff's office. Daddy got the phone to working and called the sheriff. They made plans to go to the Elliotts first thing in the morning.

When Daddy, Hank, Brother Talley, and Sheriff White went to the Elliotts' the next day, they were in for a big surprise.

* * *

The Reverend and his wife were dead.

"Delene, I ain't never seen anything like it, they were everywhere." Hank said it looked as if the cabin was a snake pit, something out of a nightmare. There were copperheads, water moccasins, and timber rattlers loose in Hibbert's cabin.

Hank rubbed his eyes and wouldn't look at me when he told me the rest.

"The Reverend and his wife were lying in the middle of all of it. On the floor in their nightclothes, with snakes all over them. They were purple looking, all swollen and bloated. Delene, it looked like they were filled with enough poison to kill the whole town."

"But what about…"

"Eva wasn't there. We looked everywhere. Daddy climbed up went in the window of the loft. She wasn't there, Delene."

I watched the tears fill Daddy's eyes as he described the sparseness of Eva's room to Mama.

"There was nothing up there but a corn shuck mattress and an old moth-eaten quilt." His voice cracked and I remembered how happy Eva was to have a room to call her own. She'd made it sound like it was beautiful.

But there *was* something else in Eva's room. Daddy found a letter on the foot of her mattress, but he didn't tell anyone but Mama about it. He thought it might incriminate her so he decided to keep it a secret.

I was at the top off the stairs, eavesdropping on them, when he handed it to Mama. And I listened as she struggled with Eva's childlike handwriting to read it aloud and crept down two steps to catch a glimpse of the letter myself.

When they went to bed I snuck down and took Eva's letter.

It was an echo of the sermon we'd heard her daddy give that Wednesday night all those weeks ago. But unlike his sermon, Eva's words were sincere.

*Dear Lord,*

*Beehold, you gave unto me the powr to tred on serpants, and ovr all the powr of the enomy, and notheng shall bi any meens hurt me. When yer sperit is on me, I am not afrade. I must beleeve that you are lookeng out for me, if I am pur, if I am a warreor they wont kill me.*

*Sinserly*

*Evelyn Elliott*

As soon as the news of their deaths was out, people came from miles around to tell anyone who would listen stories about the Elliotts. How they were impostors and thieves. They were con artists and drunks. Everyone had a story to tell about the Reverend and his blackmailing wife, and people even bragged that she'd bought moonshine from them. But no one, not one single person, had any memory of their red-haired daughter.

At first Mama and Daddy asked everybody about Eva, but they stopped asking after realizing that no one really cared.

Hank thinks that her parents killed her, and her body is somewhere on the property. For a few days he and Daddy searched the land around the cabin, but of course they didn't find anything.

I asked Mama where she thought Eva was and all she would say is that she's in a better place. They never said it in front of me, but I overheard my parent's talking. They think Eva walked into the bend where the creek turns into Red River and let herself be washed away in the swift current after she set the snakes loose.

I didn't believe it then, and I won't believe it now. I have never felt her here after that night. I think I would feel her even in death. The connection we had was that strong.

I think that she found her farmer and after they put their ten kids to bed, he dances her across their big kitchen floor and kisses her neck until she laughs. That he tells her she has the most beautiful hair he's ever seen, and she's able to forget her painful past. That she is able to talk to him like she talked to me.

I don't put a whole lot of stock in prayers, but I *do* believe in miracles. Eva was a miracle, she just didn't know it. But, when I do get the urge to pray, I pray that I am not the only person Eva has ever kissed.

\* \* \*

You know, the Hibbert's finally had to burn that cabin down because the snakes wouldn't leave. You could see them coming out the windows to sun on the porch or up on the roof. It's like they were keeping guard, just in case the rotten souls of the Elliotts tried to come back and haunt the place.

Even now, all these years later every time I see a snake sunning on a rock by the creek or slinking across the path, I can't help but wonder if he's one of the snakes that helped set Eva free.

Sometimes my imagination gets the best of me and I see one of them nod to me or look up at me with a little gleam in its eye that tells me, "Why yesssss—I helped Eva escape. She wasssss my friend too, you know."

When I try to remember how many snakes I saw Eva catch that summer I lose count. And even though they burned the cabin, old man Hibbert's field is still full of snakes.

"What kind of snakes?" you might ask.

"Big ones."

# Plans for Sweet Lorraine

*"I had no doubt that he was wanting to help her with her education, no doubt that he had plans for my sweet Lorraine, but I'd bet my eye teeth that it had nothing to do with college."*

"I'll be damned, Lorraine is gone," My voice echoed across the empty room. I stood in her doorway for a minute, dumbfounded—hell, I was going in to get her to help me set the table—just seen her no less than an hour ago. I'd run over to Wilmoth's place to take her some of our tomatoes and left Lorraine here to start supper. We were talking about how good the baby limas were gonna be with the leftover ham. Baby limas are Lorraine's favorite.

73

I seen something on her pillow, the little lace one she stitched last year with her initials in the center. Lorraine always was particular with her things. Way too orderly for someone her age, always has been. I walked to the bed feeling a sense of dread come up behind me. It picked up the letter that was written in Lorraine's perfect handwriting and noticed my hand was shaking.

*Dear Mama,*

*I love you and I'll write as soon as I can. Don't worry about me—I got a job! Brother Daniel needs an assistant and he promised to teach me everything he knows. I figured this would be a great opportunity for me, plus a way to raise some money to go towards my tuition for the University next spring. It just so happens that we are headed towards Cincinnati, so I can drop off my application and see about living arrangements. Brother Daniel said helping young girls with their education is the most rewarding thing he does. Every other man I know thinks I'm crazy to want a college education when I could stay on our dirt road and have their babies, but you know as well as I do, Mama, that is not the life for me. This way you and Daddy won't have to worry about the cost of tuition. I'm sorry I didn't get a chance to say good-bye, but I guess Brother Daniel was worried I'd back out and he said he only has my best interest in mind. After all, he is the most well-known preacher in Alabama! He wouldn't be that popular if he didn't know what he was doing. Plus he said we'd be back home before anyone missed me.*

*Your loving daughter, Lorraine*

I ran out of the room as soon as I read the word Cincinnati—helping young girls, my foot!—and told Jacob, my oldest boy, to get the other young'uns in and feed them dinner. I had to find Lorraine as soon as I could.

"We cain't eat beans without cornbread!" he said. It's a known fact that I've spoilt all five of my kids rotten, they ain't never set down to a meal without hot biscuits or cornbread fresh out of the oven. I looked into his sweet little face and didn't know whether I should feel proud or ashamed of myself. I'd have to think on that one later.

"Eat the biscuits left from breakfast. I ain't got time for making cornbread. Your sister needs me." I guess the tone of my voice got his attention—my kids may be spoilt, but they know to mind me. Jacob started setting the table without any questions.

"If there is an emergency, you run over to the neighbors, but other than one of you bleeding to death or setting the house on fire, don't bother them, you hear?"

Four sets of blue eyes stared up at me. Belinda, the baby, stuck her thumb in her mouth and took ahold of her sister's skirt. Jacob nodded and they all followed his lead.

"Mind your brother." I gave them all a quick hug. "I won't be gone long."

"We'll be fine, Mama. Shoot, I'm practically growed. I can handle them 'til you get back." He stuck his chest out, raising up on his tiptoes. I thought he looked just like Big Un, our little Banty rooster, and I wanted to laugh at the sight, but this was no laughing matter. My husband, along with most of the men in town, was gone on their yearly hunting trip, which meant that I didn't have an automobile.

I headed out the door "Think woman," I said aloud to no one, "you gonna run all the way to Greenville?" Hearing the words out loud seemed to bring me to my senses and I knew where to go. I'd borrow Preacher John's truck.

\* \* \*

Preacher John was so old that no one really knew how old he was, but his eyes still shined like a boy ready for mischief. He'd handled snakes and drank strychnine before he came to lead our little church on the hill. It was my uncle Mavis, a no-nonsense man without any imagination whatsoever, who told him that he'd have to stop all that nonsense if he wanted to preach for us.

To my disappointment, Preacher John didn't put up a fight. He's been preaching here in Ragsdale for the last twenty years or so snake free. Not that I personally wanted to take up serpents, and I certainly didn't want to watch anybody drink poison, but I could've wrung my uncle's neck when Preacher John obliged. I figured it'd make those long Sunday services a little more tolerable if someone took up a snake every now and then.

The day he baptized me in the water of Glory River, the scars on his arms from his time before Ragsdale were the last thing I saw before he dunked me under. They were the first thing I looked for when I came up, too. I realized an hour or so later that I'd used what could have possibly been the biggest religious experience in my life trying to get a better look at those scars. But I was hoping to see where two fangs went in his skin side by side among all them little white slashes.

It was the first time I'd ever been given the opportunity to see them up close and I hadn't wanted to waste it, even on something as important as my baptism. I'd felt guilty the whole summer, sure I'd burn in hell forever. That was also the summer I learned how to cuss and dip snuff like the boys, but my daddy just marked that up to my red hair and freckles, not my lack of religion. Seems like people just expected me to have more spunk, being a redhead and all, so I used it to my best ability and soon forgot about my heathen thoughts at the river.

I ran as fast as I could to Preacher John's house, cutting through our pasture to save time, cursing myself for being so foolish as I thought back to three nights ago.

"That yeller-bellied bastard!" I hollered up at the sky. I should've seen it coming, hell—I had seen it coming, but didn't realize it until it was too late.

* * *

He was a looker, lord help me. Brother Daniel was so pretty that you couldn't look at him for too long without feeling like you were doing something wrong.

There was just something about those waves in his sandy blonde hair and the flash of his pearly white teeth. The cut of his fancy grey suit made you think impure thoughts even if you didn't have any idea what it was you was thinking.

I'll admit it, I went to the first sermon out of curiosity, plain and simple. Wasn't expecting to hear nothing I hadn't heard before. Didn't feel the need to be closer to God or beg his forgiveness for anything. I went for the sole purpose of getting a look at the young preacher who was said to look like Bing Crosby in his shiny suit. Wanted to see if he was really that handsome, like one of them Hollywood movie stars. I didn't give two hoots about the preaching part—I know my Bible and I know my God—and I know that was wrong.

Should've been ashamed of myself for even thinking about going at all, but I found myself going again the next night and the next after that. Turned out he did look like a young Mr. Crosby after all.

"If you've hurt her, so help me, you weasel, you'll need all that praying to save your skin!" I yelled up to the tops of the trees as I neared the old preacher's yard.

* * *

Mrs. Thompson, whose husband owned the general store, had been the first one to lay eyes on Brother Daniel. He'd stopped in for a Coca-Cola and struck up a conversation, saying that he hadn't seen a soul in the last forty miles and was tired of hearing himself talk.

He told her he was headed to Richmond to fill in for a preacher there who was having some kind of health problems. Mrs. Thompson couldn't remember the name of the church, or what kind of ailment the older preacher was supposed to be dealing with, but she could remember that Brother Daniel had a dimple in his chin and the color of his eyes. That handsome preacher was all I'd heard about when I'd gone in to do my weekly shopping. When he'd asked about Mr. Thompson's whereabouts, Mrs. Thompson told the preacher that her husband was gone with most of the men for their yearly hunting trip in Dalewood.

Mrs. Thompson said that he looked alarmed and said he felt he should stay until the men returned. She was so impressed by his concern for our "well-being" that she offered him the room in the back of the store as a place to stay.

Well, it didn't take a dang genius to see that one. He saw an opportunity to strut around and preen in front of us women folk without having to explain himself to any jealous husbands. Figured he'd get at least three good days of meals out of it to boot. I'd had myself a good laugh at that one, but I hadn't blamed Mrs. Thompson one bit.

What could it hurt? I'd seen his kind before, he was just like all the others, only better looking and bolder than the rest. Treating us like we was all incompetent, silly females who wouldn't know how to start a fire without the men folk. He'd seemed harmless, which was ignorant on my part.

Most of the women ate it up like sorghum molasses, when truth be told, our men had been taking this trip for years and we'd all survived. Matter of fact, we birthed two calves, one colt, and finished putting up Preacher John's new privy last year while they was gone. We was all proud of ourselves, and our husbands were too when they came home and seen all we'd done.

We all knew that it was a nice break for us and them both when they headed up to Dalewood. Our men were gone just long enough for us to miss them.

I'll admit it, even though it embarrasses me now, I was just as silly as all the others. Maybe even more so, because I didn't even care to have a conversation with him, I just wanted that good looking, lively preacher to lay his hands on my forehead. *Just once.*

I'd never seen such white, soft hands on a man before. His fingers were long, no scars or calluses. His knuckles weren't knobby and swollen by years of hard labor. Hell, they looked to be softer than my own, but they were still masculine looking. It was such an odd combination, and I was curious to know what they'd feel like.

I'd watched those hands as he preached up there behind his temporary pulpit, reaching out with them and clenching them into fists to make his words mean more at just the right time. Holding his Bible up over his head to show off how long and strong those fingers were. Teasing us it seemed to me.

I thought of those hands on Lorraine and felt sick to my stomach. I know there will be a time when she picks herself a fella and they'll learn about those things together. That don't bother me none, but by God, it will be when she's ready and willing. When she says so and when she wants to. Not with some mealy-mouthed liar who uses innocent girls for just another notch on his belt and nothing more.

When Brother Daniel did finally touch me, I knew what kind of man he really was. I'd felt hands like that before—soft or not—there weren't nothing about Jesus in those other hands, neither.

"You lily-livered coward! You'll wish my husband was here

to pull me off you if you've so much as laid one finger on her!"
I bellowed as I tripped over a rock. Luckily, it wasn't too much
farther to Preacher John's or my temper would get the best of
me and I'd end up with a broken ankle and sore throat from all
the yellin'. I've been known to have a temper tantrum or two. I
blame that on my red hair along with the cussin'.

Brother Daniel had found a piece of canvas somewhere that
he used to set up a little white tent on the corner of the main
street that runs through town. Someone had dumped some saw-
dust down in front of his lopsided pulpit while someone else had
hung some garland behind where he stood. I guess it was to make
it seem more like the real tent revivals we had every spring, but
all that effort was lost on me.

I didn't listen to one word he said, never closed my eyes in
prayer. I just waited for him to touch my forehead like he had
everyone else's so I could see what it'd feel like.

On the third day Brother Daniel finally stepped off his pulpit
and came towards me. As he walked up to me, the butterflies that
had appeared in my stomach as soon as he smiled started flapping
their wings to beat the band. I felt my face flush and knew I probably looked like a dern fool.

Lord knows, I felt like one anyway. I tried to pay attention
to what he was saying, but the blood pounding in my ears was
so loud that by the time he was standing in front of me, in that
suit he was so proud of, I couldn't hear a single word. As he put
those soft hands on my forehead, I closed my eyes so he couldn't
see them. I was scared he'd look in my eyes and know I was an
imposter.

I took in a deep breath and held it, too afraid to let it out for fear I'd say something. I hadn't really known what to expect when he touched me, but it sure wasn't what I felt. I was sickened. His hands were cold and clammy, not soft or warm at all.

They brought back a memory that I'd buried way down deep a long time ago. But I guess not deep enough because it all came rushing up and took over me when Brother Daniel laid his hands on my face. I kept my eyes closed to hide my disgust and waited for him to move on to the next person.

I sat there with his hands on me and fought back the memories of that summer when I had my innocence taken from me. Those other hands had been much bigger and rougher. They smelled of tobacco instead of the fancy pomade that Brother Daniel had put in his hair, but they both smelled of the leather that bound their fancy bibles.

And they both stood over me, only this time I was sitting in a chair surrounded by all my friends and neighbors, sunlight coming through the slits of the canvas instead of being forced to kneel on the dark cellar floor.

He'd been a traveling preacher too, stopping in our town years before Preacher John came to take over our church.

"Let us pray." The preacher had made his way back up to the front of the congregation and his voice seemed loud enough to carry over to the next county. I opened my eyes then, once I knew he was no longer right in front of me. When I did sneak a glance at Brother Daniel he was looking back at me. At first he looked a little startled—like he knew what I knew—and maybe a little afraid. But then he had the gall to wink at me and I felt my breakfast coming up. I had to run out of the tent before I lost my ham and biscuits in front of everybody. As I was running out I noticed he was staring at someone to the right of where I'd been sitting. I couldn't help but notice that the look on his face was anything but preacherly.

He was the imposter, not me.

My stomach went from a hot churning pit of leftover breakfast to ice cold. He was staring at a young girl in a faded blue dress.

The sweet girl that had his attention was my oldest daughter, Lorraine.

\* \* \*

"You sneaky, slimy snake!" I yelled out again, sending a couple of mourning doves flying out in front of me. I was too mad to be startled. Poor birds, if they'd been closer, I might've knocked them out of the sky from meanness. I'd never been so mad in my life. You'd think I'd have taught Lorraine better, but there hadn't been anything to worry about. She never had no time for boys. She was always reading, always studying from the old medical books that Doc Haffey left with her. It's not like I wasn't going to talk to her when the time came. Lorraine and me could talk about anything. Or so I'd thought until I read her letter. I guess she didn't think college was something she could talk to me about and that thought made my heart hurt.

She wouldn't know how to handle the likes of someone like Brother Daniel once he got tired of waiting for what he wanted.

Hell, I had known way more than she did at her age and it still hadn't helped me.

I had no doubt that he was wanting to help her with her education, no doubt that he had plans for my sweet Lorraine, but I'd bet my eye teeth that it had nothing to do with college.

* * *

I made it to Preacher John's front porch and pounded on the door while I caught my breath. I looked around the side of the house and saw his old, rusted Ford. Thank goodness.

I thought I heard something moving inside, so I banged louder.

"Hold yer dang horses!" I heard a scratchy old man's voice on the other side of the door. Seconds seemed like hours. I was about to start knocking on his front window when the door opened.

"Preacher John, I need a favor. I need your truck for just a little while. I have to go get Lorraine." I was talking too fast and getting madder with each word.

The old man raised his hand and I closed my mouth tight to try to get the words to stop gushing out like water from a spring.

"Where is Lorraine, Cordelia?" he asked calmly.

"Well, if she ain't at Thompson's, then I'm guessing that silver-tongued devil has taken her over to Greenville." I choked back a sob, thinking about the places in Greenville where my mama used to find my daddy. You could buy liquor and rent rooms for cheap down in Greenville. She'd take us with her to

84

help her drag Daddy back home.

"If he ain't at one of them hell holes, I guess I'll find his shiny, blue car somewhere between here and there. They ain't been gone all that long."

He closed his eyes at the mention of Greenville, he didn't need any more explaining. The old preacher had been around for years. He'd seen Daniel's kind, the same as me.

He left the door open as he went inside, moving faster than I'd ever seen him move before. "You want me to come along?" he asked as he put the keys to his old truck in my hand.

"Thank you, Preacher John, but I'm probably going to make an ass out of myself and I don't want there to be no witnesses."

"In that case, take this," he said as he pulled a pistol out of his deep trouser pocket. He took my hand and place the pistol in it. "It's loaded, girl, so be careful."

I grabbed that old man with my free hand and kissed him on the cheek before running down the steps towards the Ford. I held the pistol by the grip, aware of the trigger and my shaking hands. I opened the door so fast I almost knocked myself down but managed to stay on my feet. I slid the pistol across the seat and hopped in, taking a deep breath as I turned the key.

I was lucky, I could drive anything with four wheels and a clutch. My daddy had taught me how to drive when I was twelve so I could drive him around while he drank his whiskey and sang cheating songs. If you consider that lucky.

At least I was one of the few women in Ragsdale that could drive. I could run the tractor when the urge hit me, which it often did. I enjoyed working in our pasture. Sometimes the house just seemed too small, even for me. I loved our farm, loved my life as a wife and mother. Couldn't see myself anywhere else. Guess because I couldn't dream for something different I'd never imagined how small it felt to Lorraine. Never really thought about it till now.

She was different, that girl of mine. Sharper than a tack. Prettier than any other female this side of the Mason Dixon line. She loved school more than any kid I'd ever knowed and couldn't get enough to read, not even by volunteering down at the new library. Lorraine had wanted to be a doctor ever since she read about that woman, Dr. Louise Southgate, up in Kentucky.

I'd never taken her seriously. I never knew any girl that went to college, and I'd never heard of a woman doctor. We had our share of midwives and Doc Haffy's wife was a good nurse—hell, he'd taught her everything he knew. But a woman doctor?

Her daddy and I had always thought that she'd get married and build on a little piece of property connected to ours. That was the plan. We'd picked out her lot when she was still in diapers, just like we had the other young'uns once they came. We wanted to keep them all close to us, where we could watch over them, keep them safe. The thought of her moving away to go to school scared me to death.

But not half as much as the thought of that bastard's hands on her. I realized I was holding on to the steering wheel hard enough to dent it.

* * *

86

I went barreling into town, stopping in front of Thompson's General Store. I slid a few feet before coming to a stop inches from the steps. I left the truck running and ran up the stairs, going straight back to the room that Brother Daniel was staying in.

I flung open the door, but there wasn't anyone there. All of his clothes were hanging in the closet and his suitcase was at the foot of the bed. He wasn't planning on staying away more than a day or two. Cincinnati, my ass! He was probably planning on taking what he wanted and bringing her back quiet and quick, while she was still too embarrassed and ashamed to do anything about it. I bet he's thinking he'd get a good night's sleep and then hightail it out of here before the men get back.

"Not if I find you first, you mangy dog!" I yelled as I ran back out the way I'd come, leaving Mrs. Thompson standing behind the counter looking as confused as she had the time Whitfield walked in stone drunk and urinated in her woodstove.

I jumped back in the truck, noticing a thick leather razor strop on the floorboard at my foot. I picked it up to get it out of my way and slid it over with the pistol. Seeing the loaded gun there in the seat gave me the willies and I wondered if I could use it if I had to. I hoped it wouldn't come to that. I took one second to put it in the compartment under the dashboard to keep from shooting myself by accident. Then I stomped on the gas, grinding gears and sending gravel flying as I made my way towards Greenville.

I was right, Brother Daniel's car stuck out like a sore thumb. It was parked right in front of room 12 at the Key Motel, the first place I came to. I took a deep breath before reaching for my weapon and opened the door as calmly as I could. I was trying to think of what to say or what to do, but I couldn't think of anything but getting Lorraine the hell out of there.

Through the dirt-smeared windowpane, between a slit in the grimy, dust-covered curtains, I could see Lorraine. The only place to sit was on the bed, and my daughter was on it, sniffing a bottle of bootlegged beer. She looked nervous sitting there, her skirt tucked neatly under her thighs, her legs crossed at the ankles. My sweet, innocent girl, sitting in that dirty room with the wallpaper peeling away from the walls in the corner looking as out of place as Preacher John's truck in the parking lot.

I strained to get a better look but didn't see that Brother Daniel anywhere. I thanked my lucky stars and was about to knock on the door when I heard his voice.

I rushed back to the window just in time to see past those nasty curtains as he came through a door behind Lorraine. My mouth dropped open; he wasn't wearing a stitch of clothes. Daniel was walking up behind her with that suit of his on a hanger in one hand and a beer and cigarette in the other. Naked as the day he was born.

The next thing I knew I was bursting through the doorway, little pieces of wood flying from the frame as I went barreling through.

"Mama! What...how did you..." She turned to look behind her. "Brother Daniel! Good Lord! *What are you doing?*" She jumped up and ran towards me.

"Sweet Jesus!" was all he could manage before I was on him

with that leather strop.

I whipped his bare skin with that thick strip of leather 'til I thought my arm would fall off, and then I switched the strop over to the other hand and striped him some more. He couldn't do nothing but curl up as tight as possible, because I really didn't give two hoots where the strop landed, which he figured out pretty quick.

Daniel had dropped his suit in the process of trying to save his pretty face and family jewels. I snatched it up as I backed away, leaving him huddled up and crying in the corner. I thought that maybe I'd done enough.

"You are a sinful, crazy woman!" He had the nerve to try and insult me as soon as he caught his voice. He'd been screaming like a big ol' sissy and sobbing like a child, but as soon as I stopped whipping him, he tried to intimidate me. The nerve of that man—bare-assed, huddled in a corner in front of God, my daughter, and myself—trying to sound high and mighty!

"You will burn in hell for this!" He jabbed a finger at me.

"I might burn, but it sure as hell won't be for this," I snapped back. I saw his fancy silver lighter lying on the dresser. The thought of burning fresh on my mind.

I held the flame to his grey suit and watched it burst into flames. It went up faster than I thought it would, almost burning my hand before I threw it on the bed. In seconds the worn-looking cover on the bed was on fire too.

I grabbed Lorraine and we ran out the door. I looked over my shoulder at Daniel before I was completely outside, wondering if he had sense enough to get out. I might have been angry, disgusted, and hell-bent on saving my daughter, but I weren't no murderer.

Sure enough, he came running out in his birthday suit, red welts that would soon be bruises, the only thing covering his skin as the flames leapt from the dusty curtains to the outside wall.

I heard shouting and saw a man running from the office with a bucket in his hand. I looked around the parking lot of that no-tell motel and was relieved to see that there weren't any other cars or people there. If it all burnt to ashes, it would be a good thing. I felt it was time to go. Let them two figure it out, I was taking my daughter home.

The last thing I saw as I was backing out onto the road was Daniel standing naked beside his locked car. I guess his keys were in his pants pocket. I bet he wished he'd brought a change of clothes now.

Lorraine and I passed a fire truck on its way to put out the fire and I finally was able to breathe.

"Mama, I'm so foolish ..." Lorraine started crying.

I pulled over. "You're okay, sweet girl. Your mama's here." A sob caught in my chest as I asked, "Did he do anything to you?"

"No, mama, I still thought we were going to Cincinnati to the University when you showed up. I was so stupid. Good Lord, *he was naked, Mama*!" she cried harder and I put my arms around my daughter and cried with her. Thank God I got there when I did. It was time we had "the talk," but before we did, I had something else I needed to tell her and I had made up my mind that it was the right thing to do by the time we pulled up to Preacher John's cabin.

He was sitting on his porch with an unopened mason jar of shine on the floor by his left foot and a shotgun across his lap. He stood up as soon as he saw that I had Lorraine with me and propped the 410 against the wall. I watched as he carefully lowered the hammers on the double barrel before doing so—he'd had it cocked and ready to shoot.

"How's everybody?" he called as we were getting out of the truck. I could see the worry on his face, feel it in the stiffness of his movements.

"Oh, Preacher, we are as right as rain." I looked over my shoulder and nodded at Lorraine. "But I don't think I can say the same for Brother Daniel—or his fancy suit."

"Is that so?" He looked at the pistol in my hand and I realized that there was a genuine look of trepidation in his eyes.

I handed him his keys, pistol, and the leather strop and noticed my hand was shaking.

He took the piece of leather he used to sharpen his knives and cocked an eyebrow at me, a confused look taking place of the worried one.

"You know that strop did way more damage to his pride than a bullet would've done." I tucked my chin down, raised my eyebrows, and felt a smile stretch across my face for the first time since reading the letter on my daughter's bed.

"To his pride and hide I'm bettin'." He smiled at my daughter and put his hands on my shoulders. We looked deep into each other's eyes and I knew then that Preacher John knew everything about me. I guess he always had.

Then he touched my face with warm, loving hands that

91

smelled of earth and wood smoke and all things good and smiled at me.

We burst out laughin', both of us at the same time. It felt so good that I reached for Lorraine and she joined in. All the tension and stress left my body with each burst of laughter and I felt better than I had in ages. Once we were able to catch our breaths I gave him a quick rundown of what happened at the motel, leaving out some of the details to save Lorraine the embarrassment. No doubt Preacher John could fill in the blanks. Lorraine actually piped in a couple of times and I was glad she felt like she could talk about it. Her favorite part it seemed was how I busted the door right out of the frame.

"Preacher, I've never seen anything like it. My little mama was as big as a grizzly. That snake never knew what hit him."

I ended with us passing the firetruck on the way to put out the fire.

"I'd like to hear the guys at the fire hall retelling this one. You two done real good. I'm proud of you both." He smiled at Lorraine and reached down, picked up the jar of moonshine and offered it to me. I unscrewed the lid and took a small drink and handed it back to him. He toasted Lorraine before putting it to his lips.

"I didn't worry about either one of you for a minute," he said right before taking a hefty drink.

Liar, I thought, and winked at him. He winked back and I let the twinkle in his eyes warm my soul like his shine did my belly. I knew then everything was going to be all right.

Once we got home and I got the little ones all tucked in and some food in our stomachs, I sat Lorraine down.

"Let's talk about that college, girl." I reached across the table and took her hand.

"Oh, Mama, it's too expensive. I should just be happy with what I've got and quit dreaming about that. Look where dreaming has gotten me so far."

I got up and sat down on the bench beside her, putting both hands on her shoulders, turning her to face me so I could look her straight in the eye.

I'd been thinking about that little piece of land her daddy and I had put aside for her. She could sell it. It was hers after all, to do with whatever she wanted. She'd get a pretty penny for it too. There wasn't anything for girls like Lorraine here in Ragsdale. She needed more. She deserved more.

I smiled at my oldest daughter.

"Sweet Lorraine, I've got a plan."

# The Day I Threw the Rock

"Rule number one. If it ain't yours, don't touch it."

Mama is going to kill me. I've lost another sock and the hem of my dress is wet and muddy in places. But at least it isn't torn. The last time I'd ripped the hem halfway around the back and hadn't even noticed. She liked to have had a fit over that. I was trying to be extra careful today, I didn't mean to go that far into the woods, but I just couldn't help it. There was a huge barred owl sitting in the tree by the fork in the road. I should've gone right, but he flew to the left.

You could tell by the way he looked over his shoulder at me he wanted me to follow him. I tried to ignore him, but he wouldn't stop staring. I was just going to see where he landed, I swear, but then I saw the mother deer and her twin fawns in the clearing past the pines. Daddy said he'd seen her a couple of days ago and I'd thought he'd been teasing me, but there they were, all three of them. The little ones looked identical as far as I could tell. I tried to get closer to get a better look, but they run off. Which took me to the creek bank where I saw a fat raccoon washing his supper in the water.

At least I was smart enough to take off my shoes before I chased him through the creek. I don't always remember because most of the time I am barefoot already.

My mama scolds me and frets about my clothes and hair something awful. Sometimes she even whips me because I get dirty or take down my pigtails, but it's never as bad as it sounds. She's not as mean as John Randall's mama. Lord no, that woman is the devil. The way she carries on is enough to almost make me feel sorry for John Randall. Almost.

Sometimes I see Mama trying not to smile when I come in the door after a good day of playing—I'm quick to notice things like that. My daddy knows it, too and if I'm quick enough, I can catch a wink from him before she sets in on me. I tell her if she would let me have my overalls back, she wouldn't have to worry about my dresses, but she just ignores me and tells me not to sass her.

See, I am not allowed to wear overalls anymore. Mama says that there are too many pockets and that I carry too much around in them. She'd fuss a little every washday, but never too much, about a lucky rock, shell, or feather I'd left behind. I'd always go by the washing machine to collect whatever trinkets she'd found stuck down in my pockets. But the snake, well, that was the end of my overall-wearing days.

See, once I forgot I'd put a snake in the front pocket. You know, the big one at your chest? Well, it was the perfect spot. He was scared and I think he was cold too, so I put him in my pocket and pretended to be his mother and we magically turned into kangaroos. I'd just learned about them at school and thought they were one of the most interesting animals ever, until Daddy told me about possums and how they carry their babies in a pouch, too.

I couldn't work up the same interest in a rodent I'd spied rooting around inside a deer carcass. Possums give me the willies, even if they do have lots of babies at one time and the babies are as cute as kittens. But that's another story. Anyway, he—the snake—must have liked the idea because he curled right down in the corner of my pocket and went to sleep. He was just a little fella, a garter snake no bigger around than my pointer finger. And I'm just a little kid, so it was probably the size of your pinky finger. Tiny. Nothing to get upset about.

I think that was the day I threw the rock.


Well, anyway, I forgot he was there, and she found him. My mama is scared to death of snakes. I would've never left him on purpose, I just plain forgot about him after everything that happened that day. Whew, she was so mad at me. Now I am forced to wear dresses every day with no pockets. Not even one!

At night I hear her and Daddy laughing and teasing each other about me. Mama says she's scared I'll turn out like Crazy Linda who lives up on the mountain in a cave with one hundred goats. I've heard stories from the kids at school who say she runs around naked and howls when there's a full moon. Someone said she gave birth to a litter of wolves and she's married to a bear.

Well, that will never happen to me. I think goats stink even though they are cute, and I don't think a bear would make a very good husband.

The day I threw the rock, I'd been playing with my best friend, Lucas, but he didn't want to be a kangaroo and had to get home in time to do chores. I told him I'd help him chop kindling if he stayed and played with me a little longer.

He thought that was funny. Lucas doesn't think girls should be chopping kindling—he says it's a job for a man. I'd laughed out loud because Lucas wasn't no taller than me yet. I think I hurt his feelings, but it was hard to tell. Sometimes he's quiet for no reason at all, most of the time I'm doing the talking.

I should've left with him, but I didn't. I walked on past our usual spot, looking for a good place to fix up like a kangaroo's house. I wasn't sure where it would be. I didn't think that Australia looked anything like Tennessee.

I remembered seeing a big tree that'd fallen down deeper in the woods, so I took off to look for it. Sure enough, there it was, and I thought it would be a good spot for a kangaroo den. I got down on my knees and started clearing out a place beside the old oak. I found a slew of rolly-polly bugs and a couple of earth worms. I was wondering if I should put them in the pocket for the little snake to have for a treat or let them go free when I heard some weird noises coming from farther down in the woods.

I looked up over the tree and there, by the water, was Sara Rose Jamison. She was about five years older than me, but I knew her from church and sometimes she helped Ms. Burroughs teach class at my school.

Everyone knew her, she was real pretty and sweet. She looked like a living china doll. Mama would've loved to have a daughter like her. Sara Rose had beautiful thick, black hair and bright blue eyes framed with long, shiny lashes.

My hair is orange-red, like my daddy's side of the family I'm told. I have green eyes and light eyelashes you can hardly see. I also have freckles.

John Randall, who I don't like, but try to be nice to because his mama's so mean, once said it looked like a cow farted in my face. Before I could think of something to say, Lucas hauled off and hit John Randall right in the eye. He blacked his eye good, even though I could've done it myself. Poor Lucas got a whipping instead of me. He's always doing stuff like that, and it's not like he's sweet on me, neither. He wants to marry a pretty lady one day and have ten kids. Ten. I ain't never getting married and he knows it. Plus, I'll never be pretty or a lady if it means I cain't go barefoot.

Anyway, it took me a minute to recognize Sara Rose because she looked so different. Her face was all red and crumpled up and I realized she was crying. I spied a basket at her feet and figured she'd been hunting mushrooms. I knew that's what she'd been doing because there were a couple of fat morels beside her basket. They were my daddy's favorite and we'd go looking for them sometimes. She must've gotten sidetracked like me and walked farther than she meant to. Maybe, I thought, she was crying because she'd gotten lost.

But then I smelled him. I smelled him before I saw him. He smelled mean, like the stagnant water where I find the leeches I threaten to put on Lucas when he won't play with me. But worse. The man that was there near Sara Rose smelled like a bad dream.

I'd never seen this man before, but Sara Rose acted like she knew him. I thought that maybe he'd been fishing in the creek or checking on a still. Daddy told me about the stills that were out in the woods. If I ever saw one I was to get away as fast as I could. Rule number one for playing in the woods—if it ain't yours, don't touch it. That covers everything from fishing poles to moonshine stills.

I pushed back the bad feeling I got from the man and started to walk over and help her pick up her mushrooms, tell her not to cry, but then I noticed that the front of her dress was torn and that stopped me. I got a chill up my back and felt chill bumps pop up on my arm, like a spider web had brushed up against it. I ran my hand down my arm, shook it off and started once more to walk around the oak tree. If she was worried her mother would scold her I'd tell her mine never got too mad and help her pick up the morels. I felt like I should do something since she looked so sad.

Then something happened that stopped me again.

The man walked up to Sarah Rose and slapped her hard across her face. I heard the palm of his hand as it hit her face all the way over to where I was. The loud clap rang in my ears as I stood there frozen in place.

Sarah Rose covered her face with both hands as the man grabbed a handful of her hair with one hand. Then with his other one he reached up and tore the rest of her dress open, ripping the camisole she wore underneath along with her dress. The top half of her was naked in broad daylight. She was pleading with him to stop, but he wasn't listening.

I couldn't move and just stood there and watched. I wanted to scream. I wanted to tell him that if Lucas was here, he'd be sorry.

I wanted to yell, "Kick him! Hit him in the eye!" But something strange happened. I couldn't talk. I couldn't make a sound. So, I did the first thing that came to my mind without even thinking. I picked up a rock and threw it.

I threw it with everything I had.


I have a great arm. If I'd been born a boy, which I wish I had been, then I could wear overalls every day and I would play baseball like the men do in Louisville. I'd be the pitcher and I'd win every game. I just know it. I know because I can throw apples twice as far and faster than Lucas and John Randall both, and they're the best two players on the baseball team at school. They know it too, but I'm not allowed to play anymore because I'm a girl.

The rock flew through the air, a perfect curve I didn't even know I could throw and hit the man on the side of his head. Truth be told, I'd been aiming for his shoulder, but I was just glad I hit him. It was a good-sized rock, almost as big as one of our apples.

It struck his right temple so fast and hard that he never knew what hit him. He never even turned around. He just fell to the ground still holding Sara Rose's hair, her small breasts exposed.

Sara Rose screamed then. And boy, did she scream! She'd run out of air, take a breath and set in again. I stood up all the way, but I still couldn't speak. She was still screaming as she pulled her hair loose from his hand, but stopped when she stood up from where she'd fallen and looked at me. She looked me square in the face. It seemed like time stopped for a minute, then started up again in fast motion and we took off running. She ran one way and I ran the other. We never said a word to each other. We just ran.

I ran as fast as I could. I was in such a hurry that I didn't even stop to turn over the big rock at the beginning of our path. I always checked there on my way home for fat night crawlers. If there were some good ones, I'd pick them up—which is another reason I need pockets because they wriggle out of my hand—and drop them in the mulch pile by our hen house. That way Daddy and I always had plenty of worms when we went fishing.

Anyway, like I said, I was in a hurry. I just wanted to be home, safe and snug in my bed that my daddy had built with his two hands and under the quilt that my mama had sewn for me. I wanted my mama and daddy, wanted them sitting at the table—even if I got in trouble for being late and barefoot. She hated it when I went barefoot, even though most everyone I knew at school did. She said that young ladies should wear shoes. Yet another reason I should've been born a boy.

I wanted to forget the look in Sara's eyes. I wanted to forget those tears running down her face and the sound, which wasn't really any sound at all, of her crying. Somehow, it was worse than what she sounded like when she was screaming.

But most of all, I wanted to forget the look of embarrassment she had on her face. It made me ashamed, like I'd been spying on her, but I hadn't. I felt like I'd done something really bad and I didn't know why.

When I got home, Mama was putting my plate on the table. She was in such a hurry to get to Mr. and Mrs. Gamble next door, she didn't even notice my bare feet. Mrs. Gamble was expecting her first baby and Mama was one of the best midwives around. Shoot, even Luke's daddy asked for her help in birthing his prize bull three years ago.

Daddy was listening to his favorite radio show, so he sort of whispered like he does when the radio is on when he asked me if I was hungry. I almost started crying then but I felt that if I started, I wouldn't be able to stop. I knew that he wouldn't ask me any questions about where I had been or why I was late. He never seemed to notice what time it was, except in the mornings, when he would head out to work in the fields. For that he was never late, not even once.

He had his favorite mug beside him on the floor by his rocking chair. Daddy would be sipping his corn liquor until his show was off and I could go and sit with him if I wanted to, but tonight I didn't. I just wanted to be alone now that I was safe in the house. Knowing Daddy was there was enough. I wanted to go straight to bed, but I had to eat or face Mama when she came home later. She was worse about wasted food than she was about shoes.

Before I sat down to the table, I filled the basin with warm water from the woodstove and scrubbed my face and hands till they glowed. Once I started I didn't want to stop. I scrubbed my feet and legs, and if I could've taken a bath without raising too much suspicion, I think I would've soaked and scrubbed all night. I felt dirty and I wasn't sure why. I put the clothes I'd been wearing out on the porch even though they weren't too dirty yet. I was scared that I would bring the smell of that old man in the house. Scared that he might be able to track me down that way.

I was so tired that I went to sleep as soon as my head was on my pillow, and I didn't move until morning. I was certain that I wouldn't be able to sleep and that I'd have nightmares about that old man, but I was so worn out I slept like a rock.

No wonder I forgot about the little garter snake left behind in my overalls. Poor little thing, I can just imagine how frightened he must've been after my mama started hollering when she stuck her hand in that pocket. I ran to save him before his poor eardrums were ruint, but she'd dropped him and he'd slithered off the back porch before I got there.

The following Sunday I looked for Sara Rose at church, but she wasn't there. I heard her mother tell Mrs. Dickson that she wasn't feeling well.

"Did she eat a bad mushroom?" I asked. As soon as I said it, I knew I shouldn't have. I don't know why it was wrong, but the look on Mrs. Jamison's face told me so and I wish that I could've taken it back.

Mrs. Jamison didn't answer me, but she turned as pale as a ghost. For a second she looked exactly like Sara Rose. I turned away, trying to find an escape, but she didn't take her eyes off me until Mr. Jamison came up and took her elbow. I could see her out of the corner of my eye. She whispered something in her husband's ear, and he turned to look at me at the same time I glanced over. I ran out the side door when his eyes met mine. They were the saddest eyes I'd ever seen.

I never told anyone about that day. I never said one word about that scary man, about throwing the rock, or Sara Rose's bare breasts. I thought I'd tell Lucas, brag about my pitching skills at least. After all, it had been a beautiful curveball. But then I'd have to tell him how embarrassed Sara Rose was, and it didn't seem like something you should talk about. Life went on as usual and I finally got myself to quit thinking about it.

I didn't see Sara for a long time after that. When I saw her the first time it was at the grocery and she wouldn't look at me. I didn't know why, but I was glad she wouldn't. I wanted her to forget I'd seen her crying, and that I'd seen her standing close to naked. Lord I'd hate for anyone to see me like that.

Then I heard someone found her uncle dead in the woods out past Mr. Webster's field. I hadn't even known she had an uncle. The story was that he'd fallen and hit his head on a rock. He must have died instantly, they said. No one seemed too surprised. The stories going around town were that he was a mean, old drunk who kept to himself and lived longer than anyone expected. It didn't seem that anyone liked him much.

I wondered if he was out in the woods the day I ran into Sara Rose. If he were there, maybe none of it would've happened. Surely her uncle would've stopped that man before I had to throw the rock, before she'd been hurt. Even if he was a mean, old drunk, I'm sure he wouldn't have let that happen to Sara Rose.

The next time I saw her was at church, a few weeks after her uncle's body had been found. It was on the same Sunday that I had to stand up and recite some prayer I'd had to memorize from 1 Chronicles 4:10.

I didn't want to do it. I was scared I'd forget the words and embarrass myself, but all the other girls had taken their turn and now it was mine. I told Mama if I could wear overalls, then I could write the verse down and keep it in my pocket. That way I could practice up until the very second I had to recite it, but she wouldn't budge. She told me that she purposefully picked the one she did because it was short and would be easy for me to remember.

I just knew I would make a fool out of myself and have to fight John Randall the following Monday at school. He was always trying to pick a fight with me, even after Lucas gave him a shiner, and I was giving him the perfect reason by standing up in church dressed like a girl in my petticoat and black patent leather Mary Janes. Mama told me to just be myself, after threatening me with a switch to leave the ribbon in my hair, and she promised me that everyone would love it.

Anyway, I looked up from Mama and there was Sara Rose. I'd been looking at my mama, but she was making me nervous - I could tell from all the way up at the front of the church that she was holding her breath. When I looked up and saw Sara Rose we held each other's stare as I began:

"Oh, that You would bless me indeed, And enlarge my terri-

106

tory, that Your hand Would be with me, and that You would Keep me from evil."

Sara Rose put one of her hands on her chest and covered her mouth with the other one as I spoke, and for a minute I felt like we were the only ones in the church. When I finished she was smiling. There were tears in her eyes and a look I didn't quite understand. I was just glad she looked happy. Now I could forget the Sara Rose I saw standing in the woods. I knew that whatever had passed between us had closed the door on that memory.

She mouthed, "Thank you."

I grinned at her and felt right proud of myself, but not too proud because that's not a good thing. That's a big reason why John Randall's mama is so mean, she thinks she's better than everybody else.

Mrs. Jamison hugged her daughter and looked at me over Sara Rose's shoulder and I noticed Sara Rose's father dab at his eyes with his handkerchief. It felt good knowing I'd made them happy.

I took my seat as the blood rushed to my cheeks and ears. I could only imagine how red they were. Mama squeezed my hand and beamed down at me. That was a good sign, later I'd ask about getting my overalls back since she was in such a good mood.

I sat up a little straighter in the hard oak pew. I don't know why I worried so much about reciting something in front of our church. I sort of liked all the attention. Shoot, it was worth getting in a fight with John Randall on Monday.

I snuck another glance at Sara Rose. Boy, she and her mother must've really liked that verse.

They were smiling almost as big as my mama.

# Junebug Fischer

*"I don't know what caused me to shoot the arrow.
I didn't think about it. I just did it. Was it fear or was it
pride?"*

I ain't never talked about the summer I turned fifteen to nobody except for a handful of people, and I don't reckon any of
them ever told nobody. But some stories are like dandelion seeds,
tiny little pieces of nothing to start off, but they get scattered and
take root. Before you know it, they spread like kudzu. Left long
enough and they cover up everything. Including the truth.

There's stories going around that I used to run shine and that
I killed my first husband in cold blood. You'd think I'd have tried

to clear my name sooner, but I thought the stories were kind of fun, a lot more fun than the truth, anyway.

The fact that some people say I killed my first husband—when I ain't never been dumb enough to get married in the first place—is proof that people enjoy a tall tale. I figured I'd let them say whatever they wanted. But now that I'm older, and I see that things ain't changed that much when it comes to choices young girls have around here, I think the truth might be a story that ought to be told.

Now don't you roll your eyes at me. You know dang good and well Rita's daughter did not get pregnant on her honeymoon. And you know same as me that she shouldn't have married that no count Tucker, pregnant or not. She had choices, she just wasn't aware that they were hers to make. It's a crying shame so many girls still think marriage is their only option. Even worse when people act like they don't see the bruises Tucker leaves on his wife. And get down off your high horse, I ain't saying every man is like that. I've known a couple of fine ones, maybe even loved one or two, but I didn't have to give up my life because of it.

If the truth helps just one young girl from getting cornered into a situation she feels like she cain't get out of, it's worth sharing. So I've decided to tell it, if you want to hear it.

Maury was a moonshiner, and I never thought he'd take such an interest in me. He should've fallen head over heels for my cousin Ginny, like everybody else. But then, I come to find out that Maury never did nothing like he was supposed to.

You don't need to be bothered with that just yet. But you do need to know two things before we get started.

Number one—I ain't never killed nobody on purpose.

Number two—This ain't a story about running shine.

I just want to make sure you want to hear the real story, because it's taken me eighty-six years to tell it. If you still want to hear what I have to say, I guess I should start from the beginning. But be patient with me because it's a doozy.

The whole mess started on the night of the big Valentine's Day dance at the square. Usually, my cousin Ginny went to that kind of thing with her friends, Janie and Marie, but they'd had a falling out. I can't remember now if they were fighting because Janie stole Ginny's lipstick, or Ginny stole Marie's boyfriend, but Ginny wasn't about to go alone, and she wasn't about to miss an opportunity to get dolled up.

Without me knowing what she was up to, she had her mama make me a dress that matched hers. I'd never been one for dresses, but it was beautiful, I have to admit. Ginny's was a deep pink, and mine was my favorite color, the perfect shade of blue. Darker than the summer sky, but brighter than a robin's egg. You know that turquoise color that's more blue than green? If you're lucky, and ain't scared to reach in the deep water up to your shoulder, you can still find big old crawdads that color in Sulfur Fork creek.

I'd fussed at first, but I missed spending time with my cousin. We used to be real close before boys entered her life. So I gave in and hoped for the best.

Lord, I can still hear Ginny squealing when I walked into her mother's parlor with that dress on. You'd thought she witnessed a miracle, and I reckon she did.

"Now, of course, we'll have to do something with your hair." My Aunt Rosemary said after she'd gotten over her initial shock of seeing me in the dress.

"Oh, and we'll have to put some color on your lips and cheeks," Ginny joined in, already looking for a tube of pink lipstick to try out.

"You will definitely have to scrub your nails ..."

Peck, peck, peck ... I felt like I was being flogged by two geese.

"Lord, ya'll step back and let me breathe. It's hard enough with this up around my neck." I pulled at the collar self-consciously. The gauzy material looked soft, but it wasn't. It was stiff and it itched something fierce.

"That's because you have it pulled up too high," Ginny got ahold of my collar and tried to yank it clear down to my belly button, but I stopped it with both hands. She slapped them away and pulled the neck slightly off my shoulders.

"You'll have to give it up, June. You are a girl, everybody else knows it. It's time to admit it."

None of us could stop staring at my chest. My aunt even got a bit tongue tied; then finally said she'd make some alterations.

"Well, you and your cousin used to be the exact same size, but June, you've been hiding those under your overalls."

* * *

The day of the dance, I got ready at Ginny's since I didn't even own a jar of hair goop, much less all that other stuff Ginny

112

kept on her vanity.

Ginny was already made up when I got there so she started in on me right away.

"June, if I didn't know any better, I'd think you were enjoying yourself," Ginny said as she put the last pin in my hair. I'd let her fix it without fussing or pulling away even once.

Truth be told I was as nervous as Daddy in church, and I didn't feel like talking. All I could think about was a boy named Jake. I wondered what he'd think about how I looked, because I didn't look like little Junebug anymore, that was for sure.

*  *  *

My birthday is June nineteenth, hence the nickname Junebug.

Everybody always figured that my real name was June, but it ain't. It's Helen Frances. I liked the name Helen, but nobody ever used it.

Mama, she used to call me Helen, but I was nine years old when she had her stroke and I hadn't heard her voice since. She'd been giving birth to my little sister, or trying to, but Hazel didn't make it. The left side of Mama's body, from her face down to her left foot didn't work right after that, and she walked with a bad limp. Bad enough that she spent most of her time on the porch, mostly sitting and staring out over daddy's woodshop. Mama seemed content, sometimes she'd smile but she'd quit trying to talk a long time ago. Daddy told her it was okay and carried on whole conversations with her anyway. I talked to her too, but most of the time we were both quiet.

I used to wonder if it was really a stroke or plain old sorrow that did that to her. I was so young and couldn't imagine losing a baby you'd grown yourself. I mean, that just don't seem fair at all. And she was so cute, Hazel. I saw her up close before they took her away. Daddy let me hold her while he and Aunt Rosemary helped the midwife work on Mama. My little sister just got turned around, upside down or sideways or something, they said.

There was nothing wrong with her at all, she was perfect. I know, because I counted all her fingers and her toes. I kissed her perfect ears and rubbed her sweet little chin. She looked just like a little doll. If only she would've turned back around when it was time to be born—she would've been there while I got ready for the dance, now six years old, and my mama would be singing while she cooked or worked in the garden. There are times I miss that so much it hurts, the way she'd sing, but there's no sense in wanting something you can't have.

Anyway, Mama was the only one who ever called me Helen.

My daddy raised me pretty much by himself, with some help from Aunt Rosemary. I thought he did a great job. I could out-work any other girl around, and most boys. I knew how to plant tobacco and birth calves. I could drive our tractor by the time I was eleven and knew how to change the oil in our truck before I was fourteen. I'd thought I was lucky to know all that stuff, but the older I got, the more I realized there were things that Daddy couldn't teach me. And some things we just couldn't talk about. Like girl stuff.

Ginny finished with my hair, shoved me out of the chair and made me turn around one more time before we left her room.

"Stand up straight, chest up—shoulders back." She pushed and pulled on me like I was a piece of saltwater taffy. "For crying out loud, June, help me out!"

I stood like she wanted, then pushed my chest out till the material stretched tight across my chest. I hadn't paid much attention to my boobs before, other than to think they were annoying.

"How's this?" I turned towards Ginny, expecting a laugh, but got a quick lesson in cleavage control.

"Not so much, you'll pop a stitch." Ginny showed me how to expand my ribs but roll my shoulders slightly forward as she examined herself in the mirror. I had to pull her away from posing like a pin-up girl so we wouldn't be late to the party.

Aunt Rosemary made us stop on the stairway to give us her approval. She must have liked the way we looked because she almost started crying. Sometimes she got real emotional.

"Girls, you two are growing up. I wish Carl wasn't working late so he could see you two." Carl was my uncle. He always worked late, which meant he was playing cards or shooting dice at some honky-tonk somewhere. He never worked hard at anything.

"Be safe and have fun. Virginia do not give your brother a hard time. When he tells you it's time to leave, you leave. Understand?"

"Yes, ma'am," we said in unison and tried not to laugh. My cousin Gene was in charge of transportation, but he was no way in charge of his sister. They were both as bullheaded as could be.

"Ya'll have fun and be good. Gene you keep a close eye on them, and get them home by ten, you hear me?" Aunt Rosemary called from the porch.

"Yes, mam." He answered while starting the engine. He let out a low whistle when he saw me and grinned. "Dang, Ginny. What'ja do to June? I didn't know you were a magician."

I punched him in the arm, and he busted out laughing while Ginny fussed at me to watch my hair.

A few minutes later, Gene pulled up in front of the Community Center but didn't park. "Ya'll get out. I'll be back at nine forty-five, if you ain't standing right here I'm leaving you."

"You're such a gentleman, big brother. Don't worry, we can get the door ourselves." Ginny rolled her eyes and we got out.

"Gene ain't coming?" Ginny wasn't surprised, but I was.

I thought he'd at least pretend to be our chaperone after the way my aunt went on. At least hang out behind the building and smoke cigarettes and throw dice or something.

"He never does, thank goodness." Ginny said, checking her lipstick in her little compact mirror. I wondered what her mama would think if she knew that Gene just dropped her off at the curb. I realized I didn't know anything about going out, but Ginny had become a professional in the last year. She was older than me by eleven months after all, so I wasn't about to question her even if it didn't feel right.

We'd gotten there early, which I thought was a good thing. I was able to get a seat at a table close to the stage. Not too close, but close enough so I could have a clear view of Jake, the only reason I was even there. Ginny sat down beside me and pouted because she didn't get to make a grand entrance in front of a room full of people, while I secretly thanked my lucky stars. It was bad enough the way people carried on when they walked by our table.

Everybody had the same expression when they saw me. Some of the boys gawked at me and made me feel uncomfortable, until I threatened to choke the life out of my best friend, Caleb. He turned beet red and went to stand by the door, as far away from our table as he could get, and the others followed suit.

I might've been a little meaner than I needed to, but he'd stood so close to me I could smell the tobacco in his back pocket. Ginny perked up when Billy Jenson, and another guy walked through the door. I knew Billy from school, he was one of the older boys who was in love with Ginny, but the good-looking fellow who was with him, I'd never met.

"Hi, there Virginia, how are ..." Billy stopped in his tracks. "June? Little June? You gotta be kidding me."

My neck flashed with heat and I knew my ears turned red. I couldn't think of one clever thing to say, so I sat there, hoping I wouldn't go up in flames from embarrassment. I wondered, did I usually look so bad that some person I didn't really know had to put his two cents in like that?

"You are a doll, June. Why, who'd a thought..."

"Hey, Mr. Manners, you going to introduce me to your friends or are you just going to keep talking and make a bigger ass out of yourself?" the stranger joked.

He turned then and smiled, and I had to clamp my jaw shut to keep my mouth from falling open. He was the best-looking thing I'd ever seen in person. He had coal black hair and eyes the color of green glass. His eyelashes were so thick that they didn't

117

look real. I found myself staring into them like a fool.

"June, is it?" He took my hand. "My name is Maury, Maury Graves." I still couldn't say anything, and he probably thought I was impaired.

He let me go and took Ginny's hand and I felt better. I knew he wouldn't remember me after meeting her. Heck, the barn could've burned down around the boys and if Ginny was there, they wouldn't notice.

He shook her hand but turned back to me too quick and caught me studying his jawline. I wanted to crawl under the table.

"Would you young ladies like some punch?" We must have nodded, because he and Billy went to the punch bowl set up on a table against the back wall. I watched Mary Beth spill punch down the side of her cup as he walked up to her. She didn't even notice the punch pooling on the table.

Ginny grabbed my arm. "He looks like a Hollywood star, doesn't he? Oh, I wonder if he works at a bank in Louisville. I wonder if he went to college at Knoxville—I bet he was on the football team..." She went on and on. That was Ginny at her finest, she couldn't just meet a boy without picking everything apart and putting him in a category. She had three – boys to marry, boys to date for practice, and boys to avoid unless there wasn't anyone else around. I quit listening when Jake walked up on stage.

Jake wasn't what you'd call movie star handsome, but there was something about him that gave me butterflies. He was kind of quiet at school and helped his dad run their farm. He wasn't one of the popular guys that Ginny talked about all the time, and she thought I was dumb for liking him, but I couldn't help it.

There was something about the way his calloused hands held the neck of that banjo I could never get enough of. And his freckles; he had the perfect amount across the bridge of his nose.

"Now, when they come back, you need to smile more, okay, June? Try doing your eyelashes like this..."

I snapped back to reality and looked at her like she'd lost her mind.

I mean Maury was good-looking, but he was four years older than me, at least. He'd be gone as soon as the older girls got there, I was sure. And I wasn't about to make stupid faces for anybody–movie star handsome or not.

She reached over with both hands and pinched my cheeks. "Oooooowwww," I said, and pinched her back. I had needed that pinch from her to bring me back to earth. I could stare at Jake all night, but it didn't change the fact that he barely glanced my way.

"Shoot, June, why'd you do that? I was just trying to get some color in your cheeks to take away from those splotches on your neck!" It was a problem I had, if I got upset or nervous—or excited—my neck and chest got all splotchy. I hadn't let her put pink circles on my cheeks with her lipstick like she'd wanted, and now I was regretting it. She was still rubbing her arm where I'd twisted her skin when they came back with our punch.

Maury and Billy moved the two empty chairs closer to us— without asking—and handed us our cups. They seemed too forward, and Maury knew how cute he was, plus he was blocking my view of the stage. But I thanked him because it was the right thing to do and took a drink from the cup he'd given me.

It tasted awful. I looked in the cup and sniffed the contents

119

even though I didn't need to. It smelled almost as strong as turpentine. He'd slipped some shine in there, and he'd spiked it pretty heavy. I was so young and green, I couldn't imagine why he would do something like that.

"Do you like it?" he grinned like a possum.

"The punch?" I took another sip and pushed it from one cheek to the other, as Maury watched closely. "I cain't tell you about the punch, because all I can taste it this cheap whiskey. I don't think it went through enough copper. No offense, but this is awful. I hope you didn't pay for it."

A mean look passed over his face which surprised me. I hadn't meant to insult him, I was just being honest. I had no idea that he would take such offense. Of course, there were so many things I hadn't known back then. Maury stared at me while his nostrils flared like a bull before he calmed down enough to say something.

"How would you know anything about it?"

"It ain't like I'm an expert, but I'd take my daddy's dark over this clear piss water any day."

His face turned red. "You're Junebug Fischer? Ray Fischer's daughter?"

Mine got redder, quick. Nobody called me Junebug anymore except my daddy. And why did it look like he spit my daddy's name out?

"Yeah, I'm Helen Frances Fischer, but you can call me June." I bet my neck was one big splotch. "You know my daddy?"

"I know of him, but I thought his daughter was a scrawny little tomboy." We were staring each other down. I don't know what happened, but I was ready for a fight. Maury looked like he was too, I could see the muscles in his jaw going in and out like he was clenching his teeth, but I couldn't figure out for the life of me what he was so worked up over. I hadn't snuck bad shine on him or called him scrawny.

Everybody who drank shine in this neck of the woods knew my daddy. He only made small batches at a time and used the best ingredients. If he even suspected that it wasn't just right, if he didn't get a pure blue flame when he lit it, he'd throw out the whole batch and start another. He wasn't a moonshiner, more like a craftsman I'd guess you'd say, and kept his still going to keep the art of whiskey making alive.

Daddy was a carpenter by trade and could build anything that you can imagine out of an oak tree. Everything he did he did with pride. A quart jar of his moonshine could be traded for medicine, tractor parts, shingles and if the stories were true—a doctor would take one in trade for delivering a baby—yep, that would be me— in the middle of the night. Even the sheriff and the judge here had a jar of my daddy's shine in their root cellars. He never tried to make a living off it, but he sure loved to make it. As a matter of fact, Jake's daddy had been to our house just a few days before, trying to buy a couple of cases for some big shindig he was going to have in the summer. Daddy wouldn't sell him any, no matter what he offered to pay. He was an honest man and didn't have a greedy bone in his body.

There wasn't nothing my daddy could've done to Maury for him to be acting that way, and I was ready to defend him.

My eyebrow shot up and I knew I was making that face, the

face that usually got me in trouble at school; and Ginny must've noticed.

"Maury, would you be a dear and get another glass of this delicious punch?" She put her hand over her cup, but we'd both seen that it was still half full.

Maury had looked like he was about to knock the table over, but as quick as that look crossed his face, a smile replaced it. The smile reminded me of a traveling preacher—the kind that sold creek water in a medicine bottle and swore it was holy.

"Why sure pretty lady, anything you ask." He and Billy both stood up. Maury straightened his coat and turned his smile on me. I won't lie, even though I hate to admit it, my heart skipped a time or two.

"June, what are you doing?" she asked as soon as they walked out of earshot.

"I guess I'm making him mad." I shrugged my shoulders innocently.

"Well, stop it, whatever it is, and act like you've got some sense." She turned to smile at Billy, who was watching her, then turned back to me and lowered her voice, "We have two of the best-looking men sitting beside us, trying their best to keep our attention. I know they ain't red-headed banjo players, but at least keep them here till Janie and Marie show up!" she begged.

I shrugged my shoulders and turned away from her right in time to see Jake kiss that skinny, lying, crybaby Ellie Norris. It was just a quick one, no more than a peck really, but it felt like a fist to my chest.

I had no idea that Jake was sweet on her.

122

What could he possibly see in her? I asked myself. Ellie did have those pretty blonde curls and perfect blue eyes, but still. She was a weasel.

I saw Ginny watching me watching Jake out of the corner of my eye. I tried to change the subject because I couldn't stand the way she was looking at me.

"Ginny, you'd better not drink any more punch that Billy guy gives you. Maury spiked mine strong enough to knock your daddy out. I think they're trying to get everybody drunk."

"What are you talking about? My punch is just fine."

I picked up her cup and took a drink. She was right, it was plain old punch. Before I had time to think on it, the fellas were back.

Maury walked up to us and paused to look in Jake's direction.

He turned to me with a know it all grin that made me want to punch him.

"Would you like to dance?" he asked, already holding out his hand like he knew I'd say yes.

"No, thanks..." I said

"Why yes, I would..." Ginny said at the exact same time.

He grinned at me when Ginny took his hand, then they walked out to the dance floor. He looked once over his shoulder at me and winked, making me angry and causing butterflies at the same time. Why was he making me feel so out of sorts? I'd never met anyone so annoying in my life.

I walked away from Billy before he could ask me to dance. The Smith twins were talking about their new colt, so I went over to talk with them about it. But all they could do was stare at my chest with identical idiotic expressions, so I left them to sit with Lori and her younger sister, Julie. They made a huge fuss about my dress for a few minutes and then I pretended to listen while they talked about boring girl stuff.

Finally Caleb and some other boys got the nerve up to ask us to dance. It wasn't so bad once I danced the first one. When I saw that everybody stepped on everybody else's toes at least once, I relaxed and had fun. I danced with nearly everyone there, except for Maury or Jake. Maury never asked me again, and Jake never asked me once. I even danced with Mr. Brown, our history teacher who was the chaperone for the night. He told me I looked like a proper young lady and kissed my hand when the dance was over. What a hoot.

The night was going along just fine, despite the rough start, until I ran into Jake and Ellie on my way to the restroom.

"You look real pretty tonight." Jake said. I turned around to see who he was talking to and realized it was me. I couldn't believe it. This was what I'd been daydreaming about for weeks; the only reason I agreed to come to the dance and wear this dress. All I'd wanted was Jake's attention.

But before I could think of anything to say to him, Ellie butted in.

"Are you wearing long johns under there?" she snickered.

Jake turned his attention to something on the bulletin board and acted like he hadn't heard her, while I stood there like an idiot.

I couldn't think of anything to say and felt foolish letting her get to me in front of Jake. When we were younger Ellie wouldn't have been so brave, but she knew she had me at a disadvantage. Seeing as how I was supposed to be acting like a young lady and young ladies didn't punch other young ladies in their throats.

I tried not to stomp my feet on the way to the restroom. I splashed water on my face to cool off and looked at my reflection in the mirror. That girl knew how to get under my skin, but at least I'd kept my mouth shut and hadn't given her anything to use against me. If I had punched her, I would've popped out of my dress for sure.

It was getting close to nine forty-five and I didn't think that Gene was kidding about leaving us if we weren't standing out front. I looked for Ginny, expecting to have to pull her off of the dance floor, but she walked up out of nowhere and told me she was ready to go.

I couldn't wait to tell her about Mr. Brown—the more I thought about it, the funnier it was. I grabbed her hand and started talking while we stood on the curb waiting for her brother.

"Ha! It was so funny, his moustache felt like a big fat fuzzy caterpillar..." I realized she wasn't listening. "Well, didn't you have a good time? Are you and Maury engaged, or what? You spent the whole night with him."

Ginny wouldn't look at me until I tugged on her arm.

"He spent the entire time asking about you." If her lip stuck out any further she would've stepped on it.

"Huh, I guess he liked my dress." I pulled my shoulders back to stick my chest out like I'd done at her house earlier. I was trying to make her laugh, but it didn't work, so I grabbed her hand and gave her a shake.

"Quit being a show-off June." She mumbled and pulled her hand away from mine.

"Dang, dancing makes you grumpy." I pushed against her with my shoulder, then started doing one of the dance moves I'd learned. All of them were new to me, and I messed them up, but I didn't care. She grinned and pushed me back.

"You were cute out there dancing. I was watching you, along with everyone else. You really have no idea how beautiful you are." She said and took my hand back.

"Tell me about Mr. Brown's whiskers again." I did and we laughed until Gene pulled up.

We drove the rest of the way home in silence. I figured that Gene was probably concentrating on his escape plan and Ginny was pouting because no one had gotten in a fight over her. I was quiet too, as I forgot all about Maury, and tried to remember the expression on Jake's face when he said I looked pretty.

* * *

The next morning I woke to the sound of breakfast being prepared. The smell of coffee pulled me out from under the covers, into my favorite pair of overalls, and down the hallway to my aunt's sunny kitchen.

"Good morning, June," Aunt Rosemary was an early riser like me. "I can't wait to hear all about last night."

We had fresh biscuits and red-eye gravy while my cousins slept, and she asked all kinds of questions about the night before.

126

I told her about Mr. Brown kissing my hand and about the band.

"Did you do a lot of dancing? How'd the dress feel out there on the dance floor?"

I told her I'd danced a lot, which seemed to make her very happy.

"Your mama used to cut a rug!" Sometimes I'd forget that Aunt Rosemary had memories of Mama before she was a mama; and that she probably missed that person as much as I missed the mama I had before the stroke.

"So, were there any cute boys there?" she cut me a sly smile.

I thought of Jake and smiled back. "Well, there is the one guy. He plays...."

"We had two of the best-looking young men you ever saw begging for our attention, but June wouldn't give them the time of day." Ginny walked in the kitchen and stepped right in the middle of our conversation.

"Mama, you should've seen them. Billy and Maury looked liked movie stars." She got a clean cup from the sink and poured herself a cup of coffee, filling it to the rim with milk before adding enough sugar to make my teeth hurt just watching. I poured myself another cup while Ginny talked a bunch of nonsense. I tried to interject a few times, but Ginny shushed me just like she did her cat who was meowing at his empty bowl. I fed Slinky and washed the breakfast dishes while she went on and on. My aunt took in every word like a hot biscuit soaks up molasses.

"Well, who is this Maury Graves?" Aunt Rosemary asked me. I shrugged my shoulders, but Ginny answered for me.

127

"I don't know mama, but he must be a banker or something. He was dressed in a new suit and had on really nice leather loafers. His hair was so shiny you could see yourself in it."

I laughed, "A banker? I don't think so, he was too young for that. I think." I realized I had no idea how old he was or nothing else about him.

Ginny swatted my backside. "Oh, admit it cousin, he was handsome."

"I'll give him that, but I don't know. I just wasn't that impressed." I wouldn't admit that I'd gawked at him like an idiot or how his wink had caused my stomach to flip. Instead I thought about the moonshine he'd put in my punch and the way he asked if I was Ray Fischer's daughter. Like he thought daddy would have a daughter with two heads or something.

"Well he was certainly impressed with you."

Ginny told her mama that he'd asked about me all night long. I rolled my eyes, but I did feel a flutter in my stomach. Where did that come from?

Aunt Rosemary mistook my annoyance for embarrassment and grinned like a possum.

"Looks like someone has her first crush."

I didn't have the patience for anymore talk about last night. I wanted to get home and get my chores finished before it was time to start dinner. On Saturdays I always cooked a big meal for Mama and Daddy while they listened to their favorite radio show.

"Well, I better get going, I've got plenty to do besides talk about boys."

I let the screen door slam as they laughed and couldn't help

128

but smile myself. If Maury had been talking about me last night, maybe Jake had been too.

Mama and Daddy were in the kitchen drinking coffee when I walked in the back door.

"Mornin', Sunshine."

"Good mornin', Daddy. Good mornin' Mama."

He raised the pot of coffee and pointed it in my direction. I'd already had three cups, but my daddy's coffee was ten times better than my aunt's. I nodded and he took my cup down from the shelf beside the sink.

"Did you have a good time last night?" he asked.

"Yeah, I reckon. It was okay." I hadn't thought about anything but Jake kissing Ellie on the walk to the house. Of course he hadn't thought about me, he had other things on his mind. I'd almost forgotten about it but now that was the only thing I could think of. I would've rather he'd kissed Ginny, for crying out loud.

"Just okay? You sure about that?" he grinned and pointed to some flowers in a fancy vase. They looked so strange sitting in our house at first I thought I was seeing things.

"Those were on the porch this morning."

For a split second, I thought Jake had sent them. "What in the world?"

I buried my face in a fat peony like a honeybee and reached for the card all excited. But the card read, *To the Angel in the blue dress. Yours sincerely, Maury.*

I could feel my skin warm up and knew my cheeks were bright pink. Why would I be so dumb to think they were from Jake? I was embarrassed that it'd even crossed my mind when I knew Ellie had laid claim to him. If he was interested in her, he'd never look twice at me. We were about as different as blue jays and starlings. Daddy took my flushed face the wrong way and I heard him chuckle softly to himself. I slipped the card into the front pocket of my overalls, not sure how to feel about it.

It was sort of nice, I guess.

I took the flowers out to the table beside my mama's chair on the porch where she would sit as soon as she finished her coffee. What else was I supposed to do with them? I didn't have time to sit and stare at flowers, but Mama did.

That's how it started. Even though I hadn't said a single word to him since I turned down his offer to dance, Maury sent me flowers two Saturdays in a row.

Ginny and Aunt Rosemary thought it was romantic. I thought it was a ridiculous waste of money and sent the last bunch home with them.

"Now honey, these are for you." Aunt Rosemary had tried to put them back on the table, but Ginny snatched them back so fast a few petals fell on the floor.

When the flowers stopped coming, I was relieved, but kind of disappointed. I don't know how to explain it, I guess I kind of liked them, I mean the attention was nice in a way. When I tried to explain how I felt to Ginny she only got frustrated with me.

"You're crazy, June. You have no idea how lucky you are to have someone like Maury courting you."

"Courting me?" I guffawed. "He ain't courting me—he ain't even talking to me. He's spending money on flowers that I don't even like. And I don't know anything about him."

"You don't know anything about boys in general. Not a thing. How can we even be related?" She threw herself down on my bed, obviously worn out by trying to talk sense into me.

"Maury is a catch June. How do you know you don't like him if you haven't even spent any time with him?"

The thought of spending time with Maury gave me a shiver and I wasn't entirely sure if it was a good one or a bad one.

"Just because you don't like him, don't mean you cain't let him take you places and buy you things. Look at Mama and Daddy, they ain't got one thing in common, but they've been married for almost twenty years."

I bit my tongue before I said anything about Uncle Carl and Aunt Rosemary. He treated her something awful and she just let him do it. Twenty years of that? No thank you.

Ginny had come over to borrow some sugar, but she'd been talking my ears off since she came in the door. She wasn't interested in listening to me, so I left her sprawled across my bed and went to feed the chickens and finish my chores. She knew where we kept the sugar. She could get it her dang self.

When I came around the house later that afternoon there he was, sitting on the front porch with Mama. I couldn't believe Maury was there, sitting in the sunshine as comfortable as a cat. Oh, lord, he was even better looking than I'd remembered. The shock of seeing him sitting there was enough to knock the breath plumb out of me.

"Well, hey there, doll." He stood up when he noticed me. "It's a beautiful day today, isn't it? Why, the sky reminded me of the dress you were wearing the first time I saw you. I couldn't stop thinking about you, June, so I thought I'd come by for a visit."

I tried to say hello, but I could only nod before he started in again.

"When I saw those flowers at the florist, I thought to myself – now wouldn't they be better suited in little June's hand than sitting in the window? The gal at the florist said they were the best ones they had. I said that's what I wanted, the best ones for the best dancer I'd ever seen. Where'd you learn all those moves anyway?"

Lord, he was a fast talker and I didn't get a chance to answer any of the questions he asked.

"When I saw how pretty they were, they reminded me of you." He was eyeing my overalls and my hair. I had been slopping the hogs only a minute earlier. I couldn't help but laugh out loud at the look on his face.

"Well, I don't usually dress up to do chores, but if I'd known you were coming…" I glanced at the dirt under my nails and shoved my hands in my pockets. "I would've…"

My mother turned her head towards me and smiled her crooked smile. She raised her right hand and pointed. She was right, I would still look like this.

"So, I wanted to ask if you would like to go to the movies with me tonight. I asked my cousin to come along and I was hoping you'd ask Virginia. I thought your daddy might let you go with me if we went on a double date."

Now it made sense, he was clearly trying to get to Ginny. I was just about to tell him all he had to do was ask her himself

132

and skip the formalities when I heard Daddy's voice through the screen door. "Well, I don't see why not, it might be good for June to get out of here and have some fun. Lord knows her cousin Ginny uses any excuse to get dolled up."

I spun around and gave him the evil eye as he walked out onto the porch, but nobody noticed. I might as well have been invisible.

Maury had obviously been talking to my daddy. As Daddy handed him a glass of sweet tea, I wondered how long he'd been there.

"Thank you, sir." Maury said. "Uhm mm, that's sweet. Did you make it June? I believe it's the best tea I ever did drink."

Well, he was trying awful hard to be nice, it ain't like the tea was anything special, and I knew what Ginny would say if she were there. She'd kill me if I said no. And I couldn't really say no now anyway, could I? Did I even want to say no? I couldn't think straight. I'd have to get ready at Ginny's, unless I wore my overalls. I swallowed past a knot in my throat and told him to pick us up at Ginny's house next door.

"I'll be sure to get them home at a respectable hour." He said to Daddy, and with one of those heart-thumping winks that only I could see, told me he'd be back with his cousin in a couple of hours.

I stood there for a few minutes and let it sink in. I was going on my first date in just a couple of hours. With a boy who I was sure was only using me to get to my cousin, one who had asked my daddy's permission before he even asked me if I wanted to go on a date. I didn't know whether to be excited or upset. I don't know why I felt like I didn't have a choice, but that's exactly how I felt.

I learned pretty soon that was how Maury worked.

"You better get a move on," I heard Daddy's voice from the porch, "Ginny will kill you if you give her less than an hour to get ready. If she's anything like your mama used to be, it'll take her that long just to decide what to wear."

Daddy was laughing and patting Mama's shoulder, and I felt ashamed for feeling anything but grateful. He loved us so much and thought he was making it easy for me. Of course he thought I would want to go. What girl wouldn't beg their daddy for a chance to go on a date with someone as cute as Maury? Ginny was right. I didn't have a clue about anything.

Ginny was so excited when I told her that she squealed loud enough to make my ears ring—which turned out to be a blessing, because she didn't quit jabbering until it was time to go.

I washed my face, scrubbed my nails, brushed my hair back into a ponytail, and put on the first dress she handed me. I laid back on her bed and fought back my nerves thinking about my first date. I watched Ginny change five times, tease her hair into submission, and almost come to tears when she couldn't find her favorite tube of lipstick. My cousin loved her lipstick. It was the only makeup that her mother let her wear so she had a tube in every shade of pink and red you could imagine.

Ginny didn't seem nervous at all about going to the movies with a guy she hardly knew but was on the brink of a tizzy over her lipstick. As much as I was dreading the double date, I was glad to get out of her bedroom.

134

I was expecting to see Maury and Billy in my aunt's living room, but Maury was introducing a different cousin to Aunt Rosemary when we walked in. This cousin's name was Cole.

Ginny didn't seem to be disappointed, and even if she had been, it wouldn't have mattered. Just like earlier, Maury talked so much, neither one of us could get a word in. He had Aunt Rosemary swept up and spun around so quick, we were out the door before she could remind us what time to be home. Cole had Ginny in the backseat in two seconds flat and we were ready to go.

I gave her a quick look over my left shoulder to see if she approved of riding in the back seat with a complete stranger. By the way she was batting her eyelashes she seemed to be happy with the situation. I figured she knew what she was doing. I reckon Cole did too, because I heard him tell Ginny how pretty she was three times before Maury turned up the radio to drown them out.

The second surprise was that we ended up at the brand new drive-in over in the next town. I'd assumed we were going to the movie theater downtown, a place I'd been to many times and knew everybody that worked there. It seemed strange, but I'd never been to a drive–in before and they were playing a western, which I loved so I didn't put much thought into it.

It was exciting, sitting in a nice car watching a movie on a huge screen through the windshield. I wished Ginny was sitting up front with me so we could watch the movie together, but I didn't want to embarrass her or myself by sounding like a hayseed, so I kept quiet and tried to act like it wasn't that big of a deal. I was having a good time until Maury tried to kiss me.

"What are you doing?" I leaned back, surprised he was so

close. I'd been so caught up in the movie I hadn't even noticed that he'd slid over towards me.

"Same thing your cousin and my cousin are doing." He replied, tipping his head to the backseat. I had to raise myself up to look over the seat and couldn't believe my eyes. Ginny and Cole were making out like there was no tomorrow.

"Come on, Junebug—one little kiss." He leaned in closer.

Maury was so close I could see the specks of yellow in his green eyes when the light on the screen shined bright. I could feel his breath on my face, and I pictured Jake leaning in towards Ellie. His mouth just before it touched her lips. I was curious what it would feel like.

"Okay, just one little one." As soon as the words came out of my mouth, he slid across the seat, pushed against me and grabbed my upper arms with both hands. I put my hands on his chest.

"Whoa. You have to scoot back. And you have to let go of my arms." My heart was beating hard and I was covered in chill-bumps. I heard Ginny giggle in the backseat and tried to relax. What could a little kiss hurt?

Maury chuckled and moved back a little. He let go of my arms and put his hands up over his shoulders.

"Anything else you'd like me to do? Should I close my eyes, or wait till you close yours?" I knew he was teasing me, but I didn't care.

"Well, I don't know. I ain't never done it before. I don't know what I'm supposed to do." I looked back over my shoulder at my cousin who seemed to know exactly what to do.

That's when Maury tricked me the first time.

"This is what you do," he said and then barely touched my lips with his. They were nice and soft. I hadn't expected them to be so warm.

I remember thinking, that this was okay. I closed my eyes and let him kiss me a little harder.

I opened my eyes and looked at him. His eyes were closed, and I let my curiosity get the best of me. I kissed him back. Then I kissed him a little harder and liked it. When he opened his eyes and looked back at me, I felt like I'd swallowed an electric light-bulb or something. My chest and stomach kind of buzzed, and it felt nice. So I closed my eyes and started to enjoy myself. I didn't think about Jake or Ginny or anything. I wasn't even thinking about Maury. I was just thinking that kissing was good—until his hand came out of nowhere and squeezed my right breast.

When I tried to move back away from him, he moved with me. Somehow he'd managed to get his free arm around me and was holding me tight against him. Not tight enough to hurt, but I didn't like it. I struggled to get my hands back on his chest and pushed him, hard this time.

Everything changed. His lips were replaced by his teeth and his fingers dug into my skin. The harder I pushed him away, the tighter he held onto me.

I was trying to stay calm and not make a fool out of myself, but his fingers were working their way into the collar of my dress. I didn't care what he thought of me, or if I embarrassed Ginny, I wanted him to stop. I finally got my hand free, slid it up over his shoulder and grabbed a handful of his hair right above the base of his neck. I yanked as hard as I could, pulling his mouth off of mine. With my other hand free now, I took the pinky finger of the hand that was embedded in my skin and twisted it hard.

"Get off a me or I'll holler so loud I'll burst your eardrums." I hissed in a loud whisper, sounding a lot stronger than I felt.

"Hey! I thought that's what you wanted. You seemed to be enjoying it as much as me." He whispered back and slid away from me. I straightened my clothes, too embarrassed to look at him. I felt lightheaded, and my hands were sweaty.

"All you have to do is say stop." Maury reached for my arm, and I let him hold it. I don't know why. I was so confused, and he really did look as surprised as I felt.

"Hey, do you want me to take you home? It's okay if you want me to, I understand. I won't be mad or anything. We could leave right now, I could take you back if that's what you want."

I was trying to understand what was happening, but he wouldn't stop talking long enough for me to think.

"Let me get you a Coca-Cola. Would you like a Coca-Cola?" He was out of the car before I could answer.

He smiled at me when he came back with two drinks, a big tub of popcorn and a long rope of red licorice. Maury was as nice as he could be, and we watched the rest of the movie like nothing had happened. By the time the movie was over, I wondered if it had been my fault for letting him think I wanted him to touch me. He didn't look embarrassed or nothing.

Cole and Ginny were still making out when we pulled out of the parking lot when the movie was over and started laughing when we pulled out onto the highway.

A small part of me couldn't help but wonder if I'd overreacted since they'd never even noticed what went on in the front seat between us.

I got a box of candy, more flowers, and an invite to another movie the following week. Maury had the candy and flowers delivered, and he contacted Ginny to ask me about the movie.

I ignored the gifts and made an excuse to get out of going to the movie. The more I thought about my first kiss, the more I wish it'd never happened. I was more ashamed about the way he grabbed my breast than mad about anything, and I just wanted to forget about it. All of it. Maury included.

Ginny wasn't happy about it. It wasn't her fault, really, because I didn't tell her everything. I just told her he came on too strong, I didn't want to tell anybody about how he grabbed at me. It was too embarrassing. So I lied and said I was sick and didn't want to go to the movies. Girl problems I told her, so she let me off the hook. She was a wimp when she had her monthly visit and it was the only thing I could think of.

I'd hoped that Maury would get the message and leave me alone.

But I wasn't so lucky. Maury showed up at our house out of the blue and asked Daddy if he could take me for a walk.

Just like before, nobody thought to ask me if I wanted to go. Maury seemed clueless that I might not want to go on a walk or to a movie or be felt up like a milk cow. He got out of his car talking and the next thing I knew we are walking down to the creek.

As soon as we got out of sight of the house, he tried to take my hand, so I put it in my pocket real quick. I didn't know if it made him mad or not – I hadn't looked at him close yet.

When I'd turned down his invitation to another movie I thought I wouldn't see him again, but here he was trying to hold my hand like we were boyfriend and girlfriend or something.

"Well, it sure is a pretty place. I bet you come out here all the time." I nodded and he kept on talking. "I have a spot sort of like this where I used to play cowboys and Indians with my cousins out behind our place. Not much time for playing these days, though. Nope, I am a working man. Takes a lot of my time, being a businessman and all, but I like making money."

I could feel his eyes on me, but I wouldn't look at him. I didn't want him to get the impression that I wanted him to kiss me again. I skipped rocks across the creek to keep my hands and mind occupied.

He talked for a long time, mostly about how much money he made and how much his car cost. I blocked out a bunch of what he was saying, but one word got me to listening.

"I'm sure you know about my stills, what, with your daddy making shine here, too. Well, between getting it made and getting it out of the county, I don't have much time for anything else. I'm hoping that your daddy and me can get together soon— nobody here wants anything but his whiskey. I admit it, it's good stuff, but he just ain't able to meet the supply and demand. Once we're married we'll make a fortune working together."

"Once we're married?" He had my full attention then. I dropped the flat rocks I'd gathered and looked at him long and hard.

"Yeah, once we're married. Haven't you been listening?" He

looked at me the same way Ms. Lucille looked at the little ones when they're learning their letters.

"You must be crazy! Just 'cause I let you kiss me don't mean I'm gonna let you MARRY me!" It's true I'd gotten kind of boy crazy, I guess you'd call it, but I hadn't thought of marrying anybody. Not even Jake. I tried to walk back up the path, but he got in front of me and blocked the way.

"You're not gonna let me marry you? That is the funniest thing I've ever heard! What else are you going to do, be an old maid? Or have you got a bunch of boys knocking at your door?" He threw his head back and laughed so hard he almost cried. "I'm the best thing in this town. And you are the best thing for me. We'll be the most respected couple in the county. I'll buy you dresses to wear every day of the week. No more of these ugly overalls. You won't have to go around looking like a boy all the time. You'll live like a princess..." He kept talking, but I was done listening. I tried to get around him but he grabbed my arm and just about picked me off my feet.

"Let go of me." I said and hated the fear in my voice.

"I'll let go of you when I'm through talking." He leaned down close to my face. "I like you, Ju ... Helen, and it's time I settled down. I need to settle down and I want you to be my wife. I don't want nobody else but you."

When he'd called me Junebug, it made me mad enough to see sparks, but hearing him call me Helen didn't sound right either. It was too personal, he didn't know me well enough to use it. Here he was telling me we were going to get married, and I didn't know him well enough for him to use my real name. I was feeling so many things I couldn't think straight. I was mad as a hornet at first but when he grabbed me I got scared. Too scared to talk, which had never happened to me before. He was telling me he wanted me, and I didn't want to hurt his feelings – or maybe I just didn't want to make him mad. I was so confused.

"Well, there are a lot of other girls who would be happy to be married to you. My cousin Ginny would give her eye teeth to be Mrs. Graves." I tried to be funny, and flattering, because I didn't know what else to do.

"Yeah, me and any other guy she thinks has some money. She's just like every other girl around here. No, Helen, you're different. You're the one I want." He leaned forward to kiss me, letting go of my arm in the process. I ran and didn't stop until I got to the top of the path and looked down at him. He stood there with his arms open wide, and a confident smile on his face.

I cain't explain how handsome he was right then, dang near perfect, and it made me feel funny all over again. It felt like I had butterflies in my stomach—only worse. What was wrong with me? What was wrong with him? The way he stood there so full of piss and vinegar, so sure of himself you'd never know I was running away from him. Some strange feeling deep down in my stomach was trying to take over my common sense. It was a struggle for a minute, I'll admit. It felt like I'd swallowed a peach pit that was on fire and it had settled right above my pubic bone, sending waves of heat down to the tops of my thighs. Oddly enough, it wasn't an unpleasant feeling.

"I'll wait till you're ready, Junebug. Just don't make me wait too long, you hear."

I turned and ran the rest of the way without looking back, feeling more confused and ashamed than ever.

* * *

A couple of weeks went by without hide nor hair of Maury. I hadn't slept a wink the first couple of nights after walking with him to the creek. I hadn't been back down there either. Going there would remind me of that day, and the thought of that day made me feel sick to my stomach. I felt stupid and ashamed, which made me mad. All of my emotions kept stepping on each other and I felt like my insides were tangled in a knot. My stomach cramped and my head hurt more times than not. And my chest was sore like I'd pulled a muscle. I felt like I was falling apart from the inside out.

Ginny came by the next Friday afternoon and talked me in to going with her to the movies.

"Come on June. Let's go to the movies like we used to, just me and you."

Well, that made me feel better. Ginny and I used to have fun before she started getting so much attention from boys, and the new Cary Grant movie would be just the thing to take my mind off of my troubles. We caught a ride with Gene into town, and Daddy said he'd come and pick us up when it was over.

Gene dropped us off a block away from the theater when he saw some of his friends hanging out by the drug store. We didn't mind walking the block or two since Gene was in a bad mood about losing some money in a card game the night before. The whole way there, he'd gun the motor and hit the brakes, taking his anger out on his truck and slinging us all over the cab in the process. We knew better than to say anything when he was in a mood like that. He had a temper like his daddy and could act a fool.

Once we got out of the truck, everything was going along just fine until we ran into Jake and Ellie. They were holding hands outside the theater. I was talking with Ginny and didn't see them until I stepped right on Jake's shoe.

"Hey there, June," Jake said. I noticed he was trying to let go of Ellie's hand, but she wouldn't loosen her grip. She hung on to Jake like her life depended on it.

"Hey there yourself, Jake." I said back to him. I tried not to think about the two of them kissing, but it was hard to keep my imagination in check and I could feel my hands start to sweat. I bet Jake was a real nice kisser, who wouldn't grab or push at you. I wondered if he kept his eyes open or closed. I mustered up a smile and a nod in Ellie's direction. I was determined not to let her get to me. "Hi, Ellie."

She made a stupid face, but it wasn't her fault—she just had a stupid face. Sometimes those fat baby doll lips were too much, especially since she'd started wearing lipstick.

"Two girls out on the town on a Friday—too bad you couldn't find dates. But that doesn't bother you, does it, June? I mean of course not – look at you, you'd probably rather die than to have to fix yourself up for a fella. I wish I were more like that, but I wouldn't be comfortable walking around town looking like I just finished plowing the garden. I would be too self-conscious. How

144

do you do it?" Ellie asked as she reached up with her free hand to bounce one of her curls.

There I was, trying to be polite and she had to make a rude comment. I hated the way she made me feel about myself. I'd rolled up my jeans, tucked in my shirt, and grabbed one of mama's sweaters which I tied around my neck. I'd thought I looked a little like Ann Margaret, but now I felt like a bumpkin. I knew Ginny was waiting for me to say something, but for the life of me I couldn't find any words.

I was fighting the urge to punch Ellie in her big fat lips, and for some stupid reason I was about to cry. I didn't know what was happening to me lately, but it was like I had no control of my own feelings.

Good lord, a horrible thought crossed my mind. I'd lied about girl problems to Ginny – I hadn't started getting monthly visits yet. It was the only excuse I could think of, since Ginny wailed and moaned and blamed her cockeyed emotions on her cycle, but what if I'd jinxed myself? What if that was what was wrong with me? Like I didn't have enough to worry about. I needed a minute to get a hold of myself or I was going to start crying or punching somebody for sure.

"Hey there, Helen, Virginia." I heard a deep masculine voice and turned around to see Maury and his cousin, Cole, standing on the curb talking to two other girls. As soon as we turned towards them, they left the girls and walked towards us. I never thought I'd be glad to see him, but at that moment, I was glad for any distraction I could get.

"Hello, Maury." Ginny cooed sweetly, "Why, hello, Cole."

She said, batting her eyelashes and putting her hand on her hip. I'd seen her practice that move in the mirror a hundred times. I don't know how she did it, but it looked natural, and it worked. Cole had his arm around her waist and was guiding her into the theater before I could blink.

"Well pretty lady, are we going in or what?" Maury held out his elbow. I took it and watched with a smug feeling of satisfaction as Ellie gawked at us. I even smiled for real when I noticed a smear of bright red lipstick across her two front teeth.

Maury turned and nodded at them. Jake nodded back and looked down at his shoes. Ellie stood there looking like a wall-eyed bass, quiet for a change. And I'm not going to lie, I loved every second of it.

Maury kept up the charade and wouldn't let me buy my own ticket, then let me pick out where I wanted to sit. I caught a glance of Ginny and Cole in the back row already slobbering all over each other, but I acted like I didn't see them and picked two seats in the middle of the theater. Maury sat right down and stared at the screen. If he looked at me once I never noticed. He never tried to hold my hand or anything, he didn't even put his arm on the armrest, but I couldn't relax and enjoy the movie. I couldn't stop my mind from racing all over the place.

I kept thinking about the look on Ellie's face and how good it felt. That was the first time, except for those couple of minutes after I'd put a garter snake in her desk and she'd screamed like it had teeth, that I didn't feel like she got the best of me. Also I kept worrying that Maury was going to try something. But he completely ignored me. It was weird the way he would smother me with attention one time and then act like I wasn't there the next and part of me wanted him to notice me. I almost reached out for his hand, just to see what he would do, but I didn't dare. I tried to ignore him back, but it was hard. The smell of his hair tonic itched my nose and when the music played, he danced in his seat causing his leg to accidentally bounce into mine. I was naive enough to think he didn't notice.

Daddy was sitting in his truck waiting on us when we walked out of the theater. Thankfully, Ginny had reapplied her lipstick because he was watching the four of us closely through the open window. I tried to pay Maury back for my ticket, but he wouldn't take my money.

"No, please. It was my pleasure." He said in a formal voice as he walked us to the truck and opened the door. He spoke to my daddy then waved goodbye.

Daddy raised his eyebrows and grinned, "Y'all had a nice time?"

"It wasn't a date or nothing. They just happened to be going to the same show." I said and he chuckled.

"Okay, June, whatever you say." Daddy grinned at me and winked at Ginny. Her giggle made me feel like a liar.

That's when things got complicated, but I didn't realize what was happening until it was too late. Maury had set his snare, and just like a dumb old rabbit, I'd hopped into it.

The next thing I knew, Aunt Rosemary came over to talk to daddy about me and Maury. Maury had paid her a visit and had almost been in tears, she said. My aunt felt it was her duty to talk to Daddy about my personal business. I know she meant well, since she was like my second mama, but things had gotten out of hand. I'd just started thinking about boys, I wasn't trying to hook one or nothing. Maury acted like he was my only choice and that I should be grateful. Ginny and Aunt Rosemary were both on his side now.

"I've never seen a boy so smitten," my aunt said.

"Smitten? He don't even know me," I said, feeling aggravated. It was an odd feeling knowing that Maury felt comfortable enough to pour out his feelings to my aunt.

Daddy sighed and rubbed his face hard with both hands. "I could tell he was taken the first time I saw him. And he's not changed his tune since then it seems. But now, June, what do you think about him?"

"Finally! Somebody wants to know what I think." I started but Ginny cut me off.

"What does she think?" Ginny said. "What does she know? She cain't stop thinking about that durn banjo player. Who, by the way, is probably going to ask Ellie to be his wife. A good-looking man like Maury won't be waiting around for long, and you'll wind up an old biddy. If you didn't like him, you wouldn't get so worked up about him."

"The only kind of worked up I get about Maury is mad. He struts around like a dang old rooster, probably spends more time looking in the mirror than you do." I said. Ginny, Daddy, and Aunt Rosemary laughed themselves silly.

"Well, you have to admit you do think he's handsome." Ginny crossed her arms across her chest.

"But he's so...so, aggravating." I tried to talk over everyone's laughter, but it only made me tongue-tied and frustrated.

"It definitely sounds like June's keen on him to me." Aunt Rosemary said.

The only quiet person in the room was Mama, and she held her hand out to me. I reached for it and rubbed her knotty knuckles between my thumb and forefinger.

I realized I'd have to figure things out on my own. It's true that I did think about Maury a lot, especially after he ignored me at the movie. If I was honest, I missed the attention. But so what? Did that mean I wanted his attention for the rest of my life?

I loved my aunt, but her choice of men didn't give me much confidence for taking her advice. And all Ginny wanted now was to be the maid of honor in a big fancy wedding so she could snag my bouquet and the best man. I thought about it and decided to drop in on Maury, the same way he liked to drop in on me unannounced and see how he acted. Meet his parents and see what he was like when he wasn't in control.

The next afternoon, I borrowed Daddy's truck and asked Ginny to go with me at the last minute. Of course she said yes. She wanted to see the fancy house he lived in.

"Did he give you his address?" She grinned, thinking she had something on me.

"No. He don't know we're coming." I said.

"Well June, how are we going to find him?"

I knew Maury lived on the other side of the hollow in Shale but wasn't sure exactly where.

"Oh, he'll be easy enough to find once we get into town. I'm sure everybody knows where that shiny blue Pontiac stays parked," I told Ginny as we left her house.

We stopped at a filling station just as we pulled into the small neighboring town and I saw that we could've walked there almost as fast. Faster actually, if we'd hiked through the woods between the two properties instead of driving around those winding roads. Heck, we were practically neighbors if you took the hollow into account. Ginny saw an old man sitting in a ladder-back chair, chewing tobacco at the gas pumps.

"Excuse me mister, but can you tell us where Maury Graves lives?" she asked out the window.

"What you want with the Graves bunch?" he asked, eyeing Ginny up and down. "You two don't look the type to like cock-fightin'."

He winked and I felt her jump beside me. I'm not sure if it was the way he said it or the way he licked at the dried tobacco on his lips when he winked, but he was giving us both the hee-bie-jeebies. He leaned way back on two legs of the chair and scratched his stomach, both the leaning and his large round stom-ach seemd to defy gravity before he answered.

"Go up thataway till you see the old Larson place. It burnt to the ground two years ago. The Graves place is the next place over. It's almost spittin' distance from here."

Ginny and I howled as we pulled back on the road.

"Cockfightin'" she squealed, and we laughed so hard I al-most had to pull over to keep from running into the ditch.

On up the road we could see a charred fireplace and a set of steps sitting in the middle of a bunch of weeds. There was trash all around it. Next door was a house that looked like it was about to fall down. A rusty washing machine and some scrawny chickens pecked at the dirt in the front yard and a rooster crowed at us as we got closer.

"Maybe it's the next one over," I said, taken aback by the sorry condition of the property. "This can't be Maury's place."

But right then an older version of Maury came around the side of the dilapidated old house. He was wearing a dirty undershirt and worn out denim pants over a skinny frame of gristle and bone. From all the way where we were, you could see the muscles in his jaw bulging. He looked as mad as a scalded cat, and he was carrying his belt in his hand. I caught a glimpse of a skinny woman carrying a basket of laundry behind him when Ginny called out to me.

"June! Stop!"

There was a dog sitting in the middle of the road scratching himself only a few feet in front of us. I'd been so intent on staring at the man who had to be Maury's daddy, that I didn't see the poor thing. I pressed the brake and clutch to the floor, sending gravel and dust up in the air behind us, and stopped about six inches from the scrawny hound. He finished scratching and took a second to stretch before getting out of the road. He rambled towards Maury's place, unfazed by the truck's bumper less than a foot away.

My forehead had hit my hands on the steering wheel hard enough to make my eyes water. Ginny had slid off the seat but caught ahold of the dashboard so she was fine. We were both breathing hard when we heard a voice coming from Maury's yard.

"Don't kick him, he's old and sickly." The woman pleaded.

The man reared back and kicked the daylights out of the dog as soon as it was within reach, sending it running up under the sagging porch.

The woman cried out when the old dog yelped.

I sat in the road like a dang fool and tried to get my wits back about me when the man turned towards the woman and hit her across the arm with his belt. He swung it so hard the belt wrapped around to her back. She turned away but didn't try to defend herself as he reared back and hit her a second time.

"Don't you never tell me what to do." He said before the leather made a slapping sound against her flesh.

I tried to honk the horn on the steering wheel, but I couldn't get my hands to loosen their grip. I wanted to yell at him to stop, but my jaws were clamped tight and I couldn't get my mouth to open.

"Go! Go, June!" Ginny yelled and I found that my feet worked just fine.

I went up a ways and then turned around to go back home. I didn't want to pass that house again, but we had no choice. By the time we made it back, the woman was already inside, but the man was standing on his porch, staring. The stance, the swagger, there was no denying he was Maury's father. They looked exactly alike. The man on the porch, the man who kicked dogs and beat women, was an older, nasty version of the good looking boy that sent me flowers and left me notes. I felt a shudder run down the back of my neck to the tops of my feet.

"Poor Maury," Ginny said, "I can't believe he lives there."

I didn't say nothing.

"No wonder he wants to marry you. He's probably dying for affection. And not just from you, from your whole family. He said he wants to help your daddy work his farm."

I stopped at the turn off and looked at her.

"Help Daddy work his farm? What are you talking about? Did you see his place? It don't look like nobody does any work over there. If he's such a hard worker, he'd at least put in a window"—I'd noticed a piece of plywood over one of the windows on the front of the house— "and pick up the trash in the yard."

"June, you …" Ginny started to say something, but I wasn't finished.

"Have you seen his hands? They are softer than mine. That boy doesn't know what work is. He makes that turpentine he calls moonshine. That's the only work he does."

"How can he afford his clothes then? And that car?" She thought she was making a good argument, but she was only helping mine.

"Gambling? Cockfights? Selling bad whiskey? I don't know, but it isn't from working." My head was pounding.

"Come on, June, I feel sorry for that boy. He's awfully sweet. Nobody should have to live like that."

"Especially that woman. She sure don't deserve to live that way." My teeth started chattering. She was making a saint out of Maury, but I was thinking of the way he'd pawed at my chest. I bet his daddy grabbed his mama that way when she was young

153

and naive. I bet he still did whenever the mood struck him.

"Think what it's like for Maury! Don't you know he hates it too? I bet it kills him. I bet he can't wait to get her out of there."

"Or maybe he's just like him." I shuddered.

"You can't judge him because of how his daddy acts. That ain't fair June. If people judged me by what all my daddy does…"

Ginny had never spoken those words out loud. I felt a wave of guilt wash over me and kept myself from looking her way. I was pretty sure she wished she hadn't said it, heck, nobody ever said nothing about Uncle Carl out loud, but everyone knew he owed money on bad gambling bets and gals all over the state of Tennessee and on up into Kentucky.

"Just think June, if your daddy wasn't such a good man, what would've happened to you and your mama after she had her stroke? Do you think you could've kept y'alls place up so nice?"

Ginny was right, and I was ashamed of my self-righteous rant. I shouldn't judge Maury by how his daddy acted. I immediately felt guilty and the anger swapped to pity.

When we pulled up to my house the first thing I noticed was Maury's car. The second thing I noticed was that Mama wasn't sitting at her place in her rocking chair; she always sat there in the afternoon light. Daddy and Maury were sitting on the steps with a mason jar of Daddy's shine between them.

Ginny hopped out and skipped up to the porch like a star struck nincompoop.

"Well, where have you two been? We've been waiting for you." Daddy beamed and I realized that he'd had more of his shine than usual. He looked kind of glossy. Maury stared at me, and for a second I thought he knew where we'd been.

"June took me to Sally's to window shop," Ginny lied without missing a beat and leaned against the bannister. "But there wasn't anything new to look at." She bumped her hip against the railing and smiled.

"Well, I guess I'll head home and let ya'll visit."

She turned to me and gave me a sad face, tilting her head back towards Maury. She put her hand to her heart as she walked past me. I wasn't sure what I was feeling. There was something about the way he looked at me I couldn't put my finger on. Seeing him smiling beside Daddy on our porch got me all mixed up.

"Where's Mama?" I asked Daddy.

"She didn't want to stay out today," Daddy said. "I don't know what got into her."

Maury spoke up. "I helped her in."

The thought of his hands on her gave me a jolt. As I walked past him, he reached for my arm and I flinched before I could stop myself. He let his hand slide away, then stood up and put his hand gently on my shoulder.

"I'm glad to see you, Helen. I've missed you these last few days." The way he said my name sounded like he already owned it.

I didn't know what to say. He looked sincere. In a split second, I was overcome with such a sad feeling I thought I would cry. Ginny was right, it wasn't his fault that his daddy was so mean. If anything, he deserved some compassion.

"It's good to see you too," I heard myself say. "I'm going to go check on Mama." I slid my shoulder out from under his hand.

155

It was easier to think when he wasn't touching me.

"That's a good idea, we're talking business."

"Business?" I shot a worried look at Daddy who was taking another sip of moonshine. He grinned at me and Maury continued.

"It's between us men." He patted Daddy's shoulder and gave it a squeeze. Before I could say anything else, he sat back down beside Daddy as if I'd been dismissed. Instead of getting mad, I got my feelings hurt.

I checked on Mama who was sitting in the parlor and kissed her cheek. She looked fine. Daddy looked happy, Maury seemed normal. Maybe I was making a mountain out of a mole hill.

I started dinner and thought about asking Maury to join us. My mind was going all over the place. I wondered how many times he'd been whipped with his daddy's belt. How hard it must be to see your mama treated that way. It was all so sad I couldn't stand it.

But before I had a chance to invite Maury to dinner, he and Daddy came in and sat down at the table. Daddy's eyes were bright as lit candle wicks. I didn't know how much shine he'd had—I'd never seen my daddy have more than two or three sips before. He started to say something to Maury and started chuckling before he finished. Then he turned to the chair where Mama always sat at dinner and a look of confusion crossed his face. As soon as it dawned on him what was missing he hopped up to get Mama from her chair in the parlor.

"Alice, honey. We cain't have dinner without you, can we? Forgive my lack of sense, Mama, I don't know what come over me." He kissed her cheek before he scooted her chair up to the table.

I watched Maury watch them and tried to read the look in his eyes. I wasn't sure what I saw; he looked kind of lonesome and I wondered if he'd ever seen anyone be sweet to each other. Maybe he wasn't so bad after all. My daddy sure did take to him. Aunt Rosemary too. And they weren't ignorant people.

Maybe they did know what was best for me.

I kept trying to convince myself without realizing I was doing it.

After dinner I made coffee so he and Daddy could sober up. Talk had gotten a little bit crazy around the dinner table—before I knew what was happening, Maury was talking about how happy he'd be once we were married. Daddy hadn't acted like he thought it was odd. And I couldn't get one word in the whole doggone conversation. I was plumb worn out and I couldn't wait to go to bed and put the whole day behind me. I figured it was just the whiskey talking anyway and neither one of them would remember it tomorrow. When Maury was leaving he asked me to walk him to the porch.

"Think about it, Helen. We could love each other like your daddy and mama love each other. I know I'd be happy." He leaned in and kissed me then, quick and sweet, without one speck of meanness. Was he so cocky because he knew something I didn't?

I stopped by my parent's bedroom to tell them goodnight. Daddy sat down on his side of the bed with his back to me.

"Junebug, I'm not the sharpest nail in the box. I had no idea that you and Maury were talking about getting married. I want

157

to tell you that I am really happy about it. I worry, you know. I worry that maybe I didn't do the best job raising a young girl …"

I tried to stop him, "Daddy, please, you are the best daddy in the world. And about that other? I ain't never given Maury a reason to think …"

"That boy is head over heels for you. I have never seen anyone look at someone the way he looks at you."

"But Daddy, he's pushy. He's bossy. I …"

"He's a young buck, Junebug. He just needs to be trained. I wish you could ask your Mama about how I was when I was young. I cussed too much and fought too much. Sometimes I took your Mama's feelings for granted."

"Daddy, it's not the same. I don't much like him most of the time. And how can he be so in love with me, when he doesn't even know me?"

Daddy sighed and closed his eyes. I gathered that the coffee hadn't had as much of an effect as I'd hoped. "I know girls usually talk about this kind of thing with their mamas and it might be a   bit embarrassing to talk to me, but it's okay. You're growing up, Junebug. You know I'm getting older every day. I used to wonder what it would be like when you grew up and got married and moved away. I've been selfish, I reckon, 'cause I only think about how much I'll miss you. I don't think about your life. But now Maury shows up and I guess it's time for me to start thinking about it. You'll want to start your own family one day."

I took a few steps in the room so I could see his face. I noticed for the first time the wrinkles around his eyes and the gray hair on his temples.

"You feeling okay, Daddy?" I asked.

"I'm fine, hon, just had too much whiskey. I'll feel better in the morning." He sounded tired and embarrassed.

"I wasn't going to say anything, but since you brought it up, what got into you? I ain't never seen you drink that much before." I laughed and pushed his shoulder, trying to make him smile.

"That Maury, he's got a gift for talking, don't he? He should be a preacher." He chuckled "Or a salesman. He asked me to have a drink with him and the next thing I knew I was ready to open another pint. Thank goodness I had enough sense to stop when I did."

"Yeah, he can be pretty convincing. Good night, Daddy. I'll see you in the morning."

I went to my room with the sound of Aunt Rosemary and Ginny singing Maury's praises in my head, and the memory of him sitting with us as a family for dinner. I'd never thought about having kids of my own, but that night I dreamt I had a baby that looked just like Hazel.

The next afternoon I was picking tomatoes at the side of the house when Maury's car pulled up and parked in the driveway. I'd been thinking all night and most of the morning about what it would be like to marry Maury. I'd almost convinced myself that it would be a good thing; almost convinced myself that he needed me and my parents to show him what a family was supposed to be. He got out his car and I noticed someone was with him.

"Hello, Helen. Is your daddy home?" Maury asked without saying anything about how pretty I was or how good it was to see me. I looked from him to the skinny, coarse looking man standing beside him and felt a shiver run down my spine. Even though the man was dressed in clean clothes and looked fresh shaved, he still looked dirty.

Before I could answer, Maury continued, "We're here to talk some business with your daddy. Why don't you go find him and bring us some tea? We'll have a seat on the porch."

I felt a sudden flash of anger wash over me and was about to tell him what he could do with his tea when Daddy stepped outside

"Good afternoon, boys. What can I do for you?" Daddy asked.

"This here is my cousin, Ferron, the one I was telling you about last night. We've got a proposition for you. I was wondering if we could get a sample of whiskey and have a conversation."

I was fuming. First, I was furious at the way he ordered me around, but secondly I was mad at myself for even thinking about taking his words seriously. I couldn't stand him, why did I care what other people thought? I carried the basket of tomatoes to the back porch where Mama was sitting so I wouldn't have to go near Maury or his cousin. The look on Mama's face stopped me short.

"What is it, Mama?" I asked, "You want some tea?"

She raised her good hand and touched my arm. I patted it and leaned down to kiss her. Mama touched my face and tried to say something. I hadn't seen her try so hard to speak in a long time. The best she could do was make a moaning sound that just about broke my heart.

"What is it? Are you getting chilly?" I tucked a quilt around her legs and went to get her a glass of tea. I needed a minute to straighten my face. When I came back, I noticed a tear running down her cheek. It spooked me for a second, but then I realized it was on the left side of her face and was probably plain old water from her eye and not a tear. I wiped it away and went in to start dinner. I was scared if I stayed out there with her I'd start crying myself, and she'd think I thought she was pitiful. She couldn't stand anybody feeling sorry for her.

We'd need eggs for the cornbread, so I went around the back of the house, unnoticed, to check on the hens. They hadn't laid any eggs that morning, but hopefully there'd be one or two in there now or I'd be stuck making biscuits. I heard voices from the front porch, and I tried my best to pay them no mind, but then I heard something I couldn't ignore. I crept up to the corner of the house so I could hear Maury and Ferron's conversation better.

"How much has he got stashed away, you reckon?"

"I'm not sure exactly, but shit, Ferron, even if it's only one case, we can turn that into three cases easy. Me and the old man got a good still hidden back behind our house. We're down to one after those chicken shit government men busted up the two over on the other side of Shale, but it's putting out pretty regular. We use what we got to extend Fischer's shine I'm thinking..."

"Aw, hell, Maury. That still behind your house needs to be torn down too."

"Shit, no! It's in the perfect place. They've been trying to pin us to stills all the way over in Hickman County. They'll never look in our backyard." Maury sounded pleased with himself.

"Last time I seen it, it was full of rust and who knows what.

You're lucky you ain't killed nobody yet with that panther piss." Ferron said.

Maury laughed, not the least bit ashamed. He didn't even try to deny it. "Well, ain't nobody died yet. And if we mix it with Fischer's whiskey we can sell it for twice as much with half the risk."

I hurried to the henhouse, not sure if I could bite my tongue any longer and almost ran into Daddy as he was coming out. He had a jar of moonshine in his hand and a grin on his face.

"Well, no wonder the hens ain't layin'—they're drunk." I said, and Daddy laughed. I never knew where he kept his whiskey hidden until now. He pulled three eggs out of the bib pocket of his overalls.

"Looky what I found." He handed them over.

"Daddy, what are Maury and that guy doing here?"

"I'm not right sure, hon, but I aim to find out."

"I don't like it. I heard them…" I expected an argument and was trying to talk fast before he could stop me. But he surprised me by agreeing.

"Me neither. I'll be in to make you and your mama that cornbread, June. I'll give them boys a sip of whiskey and send them on their way. Don't you worry about it. Just stay inside and let me take care of it, okay?"

I knew my daddy wasn't no fool. I turned and ran back to the house feeling better than I had in a while. Mama was sitting in her chair with our big barn cat, Tiny, on her lap. He was a good mouser but not one to take any petting except from Mama. He didn't move a muscle when I stepped onto the porch, but Mama looked up and I saw that she was crying real tears.

"What's the matter, Mama? Don't you cry, now. We're going to have some of Daddy's cornbread for dinner. He's going to make it himself—your favorite."

I dried her face and went inside, and I told myself that it had to be something in the air that was making her eyes water. I couldn't stand the thought of her crying and not being able to tell me why.

I jumped when I heard a booming voice from out front. I stopped what I was doing and tiptoed into the parlor to peek out the window. Ferron was standing just a couple of feet in front of Daddy and his face was the color of a radish.

"My cousin was under the impression that you wanted to go into business together." Ferron said.

"I don't know what would've given him that idea. I ain't never had the slightest interest in getting in the moonshine business. I like to have a little on hand to clear up a cough or ..."

"Bullshit. Look at this place you got here. You telling me that you never sold moonshine to make money?"

Daddy stood up then. "This house was my daddy's house, and his daddy's before that. Any money I make is from the crops and the livestock I raise, or the furniture I build. Honest work. But I'm guessin' neither one of you know much about that. My granddaddy served time for selling moonshine, and that never seemed like something I'd be interested in. Everybody around here knows that."

"Wait just a minute," I heard Maury's voice, but I couldn't see him from my place at the window. "It seems like we all got off on the wrong foot. My cousin can be a tad dense, Mr. Fischer, he purely misunderstood. Why, once me and June are married, I'll be working right alongside of you, I'll be sweating and plowing and ..."

I waited to hear what he would say, but he couldn't think of anything else. Of course he couldn't! I'd been right, and he didn't have a clue what a working man's day was like.

"That's another thing, Maury. I'm not sure that she wants to get married anytime soon."

"She doesn't know what she wants, because that sure ain't what she's been telling me."

I almost fell out at the bald faced lie, but Daddy's voice kept me on my feet.

"That's enough. I need to get inside and give my daughter a hand in the kitchen. Ferron," Daddy nodded towards him and reached out. Ferron thought he was trying to shake his hand, and bowed up to try to intimidate him, but Daddy ignored him and reached for the mason jar he was holding.

"I hope I made it clear that I do not want to do business with you or your cousin." I watched as Daddy and Ferron stared each other down. My daddy took the jar out of Ferron's hand without blinking and I saw a glimpse of the man that I'd only heard stories about.

"And Ferron, if you ever come back to my place again, I'll fill your backside with buckshot."

Maury stood up then and I saw him reach out to take Daddy's hand, but Daddy wouldn't take his eyes off Ferron. Maury ran his hands through his hair and looked like he was trying to think of something else to say. He finally gave up and got in his car without another word.

Daddy stood on the porch until they were gone. I opened the door, stepped out beside him, and gave him a hug. I knew Maury's cousin hadn't come up with that idea all on his own, but I held my tongue because I didn't want to make Daddy mad again, and I was tired of thinking about Maury. I knew for a fact he was a lowdown lying dog, and I was finished wasting my time on the likes of him. And after what just happened I thought Maury was as good as gone so there wasn't no sense in bringing it up.

"Come on Daddy, I got the skillet ready for you." I tugged the sleeve of his shirt until he came inside.

But I'll be danged if the next day Maury came by with more store bought flowers in a vase for me and Mama.

"I'm not here to visit," Maury said as soon as he got out of his car, "I just come to apologize to your daddy."

"Oh. I reckon them flowers are for him then." I said.

"Don't be stupid. These are for y'all." He stretched out as if to hand them to me, but I ignored them.

"What would you be apologizing for?" I asked, hoping he would say something about that Ferron fella. I was ready to let loose.

"It's between us men, Helen." was all he said. He didn't have the sense to know that I knew what happened.

Maury put the vase on the table beside Mama's rocker and acted like he was going to sit down. I stopped him before he could make himself comfortable and moved to sit in the empty seat instead but neither one of us could sit and we were standing toe to toe. I felt stronger with Mama there beside me.

"Well, you'll have to come back later. It's only us women here right now."

I saw the muscles in his jaw bulge and was ready for an argument, but he left without saying goodbye, his charm and manners forgotten.

I sat down beside Mama and watched her shake her head back and forth.

"You don't like him, do you, Mama?" I asked, more to myself than anything. She surprised me by knocking the flowers off the small table onto the floor. I jumped when the glass shattered and looked at her closely.

She worked to say something, but nothing came out. She clenched her fist and shook it in the direction of the dust clouds Maury's car had kicked up.

"I hear you Mama, loud and clear!" I got up and hugged her tight before I picked up the pieces of broken glass and kicked the flowers off the porch into the yard.

I swear, if I didn't know any better Mama smiled a full smile at me.

It was a few days later that Maury stopped back by. We'd finished supper but there was still some sunlight left. Daddy was on the porch beside Mama sharpening his knives, and I was weeding out the flowerbeds.

"That boy is about as dense as a brick." I said and Daddy chuckled.

Maury parked his car. Then he got out and walked slowly towards the porch.

"Hello, Helen." He said looking like stray dog with his tail between his legs, "I'd like to speak to your Daddy alone."

Daddy spoke up, "You can say whatever you want to say in front of June and Alice."

I stood my ground and watched as Maury kicked at the dirt for a minute. It was obvious he wanted me to leave, but I wasn't going nowhere.

He cleared his throat before he started talking. "I wanted to apologize for Ferron's behavior." You could barely hear him at first, but he found his voice, "I swear I don't where he got that crazy plan of his. I didn't have any idea that he was going to say any of that stuff.

"Mr. Fischer, I was as surprised as you. I'm sorry he was so disrespectful. I should've known better than to bring him by, it's just that I was telling him how good your whiskey was and all. I ain't been around him much since we were little kids, I didn't know he'd turned into such a conniving person."

If I hadn't known better I would've believed every word. Daddy had been right when he said Maury would make a good preacher, he'd be one of those smooth talking ones that could convince the poorest of families to put their last fifty cents in the offering plate. But I had heard the two of them talking when Daddy wasn't there with my own ears. I knew Maury was full of horse crap.

"I hope you don't hold it against me. And I wanted to offer to help you around here, you know, if you need an extra hand." He put on a good show, I'll give him that, running his hand through his hair and shuffling his feet.

I felt a grin coming and was just about to give him an earful. But what he said next knocked the words right out of my mouth.

"I'll get on my way, let you think about it. Just know that I wouldn't do anything to disrespect you or your daughter. I love her, Mr. Fischer, and I want you to know that."

Then Maury got in his car and left without saying anything to me. He'd just said that he loved me – not to me, to my daddy – like it was the most normal thing in the world. He'd never once told me that. Oh, he told me he wanted to marry me, that he chose me – but he'd never said he loved me.

I'd watched how Daddy's grip loosened on the leather strap he was holding to sharpen the blades as Maury stood there giving his sermon and I wanted to scream. Surely he wasn't falling for it.

Damn it all to hell. I had to do more than talk to get anyone to listen. I needed proof to back up what I'd overheard of Ferron and Maury's conversation on the porch. I needed it for myself as much as anything, because even though I hated to admit it, Maury got me turned upside down and sideways.

The presents, the attention, the flattery, not to mention the way he made me feel. My body seemed to have a mind of its own and my common sense was fighting a losing battle. I needed Mama's advice, but she couldn't give it. There was no way I could talk to Daddy about what I was feeling. I was too embarrassed and didn't understand enough about what it was I was feeling to even try. Ginny and Aunt Rosemary had already told me what they thought, but as much as I loved them both, neither one of them had the sense God gave a goat when it came to men. I was on my own.

I decided that night while I was trying to fall asleep that I was going to go looking for Maury's still and see for myself what it was like. If it was in the same condition as his daddy's house; and I had some strong facts to back up my misgivings and not just bits and pieces of what I'd heard, then Daddy would listen to what I was saying without thinking I was just a love-struck girl who was flustered by Maury's attention.

The next day I told Daddy I was going hunting in the woods behind our place. It was a good excuse since I loved to hunt. Well, I loved to look for things to hunt more than I liked the actual killing part. I never learned to like shooting a gun. But I'd been hitting bull's eyes with my bow since I was nine.

I took my bow and a few arrows with me for a cover, feeling kind of foolish. I wasn't sure what I hoped to find exactly, I just knew I had to do something instead of waiting on Maury to come back around with more stories.

I took off in the direction that would take me to the back of the Graves's property and it wasn't long before I found what I was looking for. I tried to imagine Maury and his cousins playing down there as kids but couldn't picture it. The only playing Maury ever did with his relations was probably stealing tomatoes from their neighbor's gardens.

Standing at the top of a ridge looking down into a ravine where a natural spring poured down the rock face into a small pool, I heard voices and smelled wood smoke. I knew there would be a still somewhere. I spotted it under a rocky ledge and

169

admired the way it blended in with the rocks and tree limbs. It would've been a pretty picture if not for the rusted lines and trash all around. They kept the still like they kept their house. Not one bit of pride in keeping it up, plus they used an old radiator as a condenser. That was pure laziness. It was a proven fact that you couldn't get clean whiskey that way. All it was good for was rot gut and yella eyes.

Sprawled out on the ground beside the still, was a scrawny man in filthy clothes. I was afraid he was dead, the way he was just lying there on the ground, but before I could figure that out, I spotted Ferron not too far away.

Then I heard a vehicle pulling up to the still from the other side of the hollow. It was a truck, and the man I'd seen beating his wife with a belt was behind the wheel. I looked closer and saw Maury in the passenger seat. They parked and Maury's daddy got two metal cans out of the back of the truck that looked like the ones we used to carry kerosene. He carried them towards Ferron and set them on the ground. I couldn't make out what they were saying, so I left the bow and arrows behind the tree where I was hiding and made my way down a little further as quiet as possible. I was able to hide behind a big boulder twenty feet further down the ravine.

I listened as the men all cussed and argued with each other. Maury's daddy was mad about something, and Ferron was arguing with him. Every once in a while I could hear Maury pipe in, but it was clear that the old man ran the show. My stomach tied up in knots when I understood what they were saying. It was even worse than I'd expected.

He was mad at Maury for not getting his hands on my daddy's moonshine. "You still don't know where he has his still? What the hell have you been doin' all this time? If you'd keep your pecker in your pants and quit sniffin' around his girl, we'd be set by now."

"Daddy, you're the one that told me that marryin' June was the way …"

I felt a jolt when I heard my name.

"Marryin' her, yeah. Courtin' her, no. Once you two tie the knot, you can pet on her all you want. Right now we need to be takin' care of business. What's yer problem, boy? You gone soft on me?"

"She's different, I ain't never had to work so hard to get a piece of tail in all my life, but she's coming around. Her daddy likes me, I can tell." Maury said and Ferron laughed.

"I don't give a goddamn what her daddy thinks about you, once yer family, he'll have to like you. She's his only young'un, you jackass. It's a given. We're runnin' out of time, those damn revenuers 'bout broke me. And I ain't going back to Fulsom." Maury's daddy was yelling now.

"I don't know where his still is, but I got a good idea where he keeps his stash." Maury took a step back from his daddy who'd gotten so close he was almost standing on his son's toes.

"Then you need to quit fartin' around and get it. Steal it if you have to, I don't give a good goddamn. We ain't got much time before all of our whiskey is gone and then we're going to be flat broke."

Maury's daddy noticed the man lying on the ground and ran

171

up to him.

"Jesus, Lonnie. You been drinking all day?" He yelled before he kicked the man in the side.

The man called Lonnie sat up but couldn't stand. After several attempts he crawled to a tree trunk and pulled himself up to a sitting position.

"You jake-leg son of a bitch," Maury's daddy yelled again.

"I cain't see. Hey, I cain't see!" the man beside the stump cried out.

"This ignorant owl fucker done went and drunk hisself blind," Ferron said.

"Jesus H. Christ. This's all I need right now. Didn't we tell him not to drink this batch? Didn't we tell him? Lonnie, you goddamn idgit—this was to be cut with Fischer's shine when my no good son gets off his lazy ass and brings it to me." He kicked at Lonnie, missed, and turned to Ferron and Maury, "This ain't good, boys. Shit fire, this ain't no good at all."

Maury didn't argue or make any comment.

"Take him out of here. Get him as far from here as you can and put the old bastard out of his misery."

"You mean...?" Maury asked.

"Hell, yes, that's what I mean. He ain't gonna get no better—as much as he's drank—and we'd all go to prison if people start asking questions. All of us, not just me. You two are as tied up in this as I am, and I ain't takin' the fall by myself this time, Ferron. Hell no, you lyin' sack of shit, this is as much you as me." He looked at his son and said, "And as much us as you. You wanted to be a big moonshiner? Well, here you go. Take care of Lonnie

172

and don't come back until you've got Fischer's shine with you."

I couldn't hear what else they were saying. The blood was pounding in my ears, blocking out everything else. I had to take some deep breaths to calm myself down. I knew what I'd find would be bad – but I had no idea it would be this bad. I watched as they pulled Lonnie to the truck, dragging him through the leaves and dirt and I wondered how much poison he'd drunk.

I'd bet my lucky buckeye that if you lit a match to that so-called moonshine, it'd flare up red. What was it Daddy used to tell me? Lead burns red and makes you dead.

I got my nerves settled and decided I'd seen enough. I need-ed to tell Daddy what I saw, tell him about Lonnie. I was halfway back to where I'd laid my bow and arrows when a bad feeling come up on me. I looked back over my shoulder, but Maury's daddy wasn't at the still. I turned and looked all around the bot-tom of the ravine for him. He'd stayed behind, I was sure of it, but I couldn't see him anywhere.

Then I heard him, a minute too late, come up from the right. I tried to run up the ravine, but it was steep, and I lost my footing. I slipped and came down hard on my knees. He moved more like a polecat than human and was on me so fast that he had me turned over, flat on my back, before I knew what was happening.

Sweat was streaming down his face. He raised his hand and slapped me hard before straddling me. I froze, too scared to move even if I could have. I figured once I told him I was deer hunting, he'd let me go. But I didn't get the chance. I started to tell him, and he slapped me again—this time busting my lip.

"Shut yer fuckin' mouth. I know who you are, you sneaky

little bitch. What're you doin' up here? You a lookout for yer daddy?" He was leaning into me, squeezing the air out of my lungs. I tried to answer but all I could do was shake my head. He grabbed a handful of my hair and brought his face closer to mine.

"You sure did turn out to be a pretty youngun. No wonder my son don't know if he's a comin' or goin'." He put his nose in my hair and took a deep breath. "Uhm, huh. And you smell pretty too."

That's when he tried to put his tongue in my mouth and I found a strength in me I hadn't known existed.

I slapped him with my right hand and punched him in the eye with my left fist. I started kicking and clawing and almost had him off me when he hauled off and hit me with a fist that felt like a hammer. I was dazed for a second. Stars danced in front of my eyes and it felt like I was falling, but I came to and started fighting as soon as he tried to kiss me again.

"Yer one feisty little heifer, ain't ya." He actually smiled as he slapped my face again.

After hitting me a couple of times in the ribs, and knocking the air completely out of me, he managed to get my arms pinned under his knees. He unbuckled his belt and slid it out of the loops. I imagined him whipping me like I'd seen him hit his wife. I fought with everything I had left trying to get my hands free, bucking and kicking. I wasn't going to just lay there and let him whip me but he had other plans for the belt. He looped it around my neck and slipped the end through the buckle.

I gave one big heave and raised my hips off the ground a couple of inches. I almost got my hands free when he pulled the belt as tight as it would go around my neck. I couldn't breathe and all the fight went out of me. He was panting and drooling and rubbing his hips up against me.

"You like that, dontcha? I can tell. No wonder my son wouldn't ever tell me about you. He wanted to save you all for hisself. Well, that's all fine and good, he can have you when I'm through."

I felt something in his pocket, something hard and hot and wondered if he had a pistol, but then the realization of what was about to happen struck me and I would've vomited if not for the strap of leather cutting into my throat.

"You relax, little miss, and I'll make this a time you'll never forget. You'll be beggin' for more by the time I'm finished. My son said he ain't never had such a hard time trying to get a piece a tail, but he was goin' about it the wrong way. You need a real man to show you what you want." His sweat dripped onto me in greasy drops. The most I could do was turn my head to keep it from falling on my face.

He struggled to get the zipper of his pants down, but it was stuck on the tail of his shirt that was tucked inside of his dirty blue jeans. The belt was so tight around my neck that I started to see sparks shoot across my vision and things went gray around the edges. I willed myself not to pass out—I knew I had to stay awake no matter what.

When he let go of the belt to use both hands on his zipper, the tension slacked between it and my neck, allowing me to get some air. I gulped in as much as I could, at the same time trying to figure out how to get out of the mess I'd gotten into. No one would hear me if I screamed—there weren't any houses other than Maury's close by.

"Unbutton yer shirt, you snivelin' bitch. Show me them little titties you got and I won't choke you again."

He was still working on his zipper, panting and red-faced, the bulge in his pants pushing against the fabric. I didn't want to unbutton my shirt, but I didn't want him to suffocate me either. I slid my hands out from under his knees and put them on my chest.

There was something sharp digging into the back of my head that I hadn't noticed before. I hadn't felt anything but his slapping and punching but now I could feel the pain at the base of my skull.

"Goddamnit!" he finally gave up trying to pull the fabric out of his zipper and started working on pulling the zipper out of his pants. He looked like animal straining to get free from a trap. His pants were old and worn thin and I could see the stiches straining around the zipper starting to give way.

"I said, unbutton yer shirt or I'll choke the livin' shit out of you. Don't make me no difference if yer passed out or not." The sound of his voice was like another slap to the face.

That's all I needed to make up my mind on what to do next. With my left hand, I undid the top button which kept his eyes off of my right hand. I slid my right hand behind my head and felt for the rock that was underneath me.

I don't know if I'll ever get the look he had on his face out of my mind. The way he licked his lips when my button came undone shook me, but only for a second.

While my left hand kept his gaze on my chest, my right hand grasped the rock. I wrapped my fingers around it as tight as possible and I swung it at his face with all of my might.

I felt something snap and his nose flattened against the rock as it made contact with the center of my target. I felt teeth break and skin split and I kept pushing the rock after the force behind the swing stopped. I heard a scream and wasn't sure if it was from him or me.

He fell off of me and I was up and running without looking back, I heard him screaming and cussing, but I didn't look to see if he was following me. I made it to the place where I'd left my bow and arrows and grabbed them. I stopped only long enough to get his belt from around my neck.

I fought back tears as the leather strap tightened in the buckle instead of loosening, but I willed myself to calm down and was able get free. I flung the belt that felt more like a living breathing thing—like a writhing copperhead with fangs, instead of a piece of dead cowhide—as far as I could away from me.

Once I made it to the top of the ridge, I turned around to see him stumbling down the ravine in the opposite direction, heading towards his still.

I don't know why I did what I did next.

I don't know what caused me to shoot the arrow. I didn't think about it. I just did it.

Was it fear or was it pride?

Was it both? I set my sight on the still and let the first arrow fly. It hit the top of the still where the steam was built up and I could see it billow up into the air. Knowing I put a hole through that rusty piece of trash felt powerful. I aimed another one at the radiator. I hit my mark within an inch of the target. More hissing and more steam.

I heard Mr. Graves cuss and watched as he threw himself a good fit, while he held his face and kicked and screamed, staggering around like he was half blind and crazy. I thought of the man they called Lonnie.

He kicked one of the metal cans into the fire underneath the still, while he cussed everything under the sun. I should've left then, but I wanted to put one more hole in his sorry excuse for a still. I set my sight, pulled back my arrow, and let it fly, but before I saw where it hit there was a loud explosion and a wall of fire shot up dang near fifteen feet. I saw Mr. Graves enveloped in flames. If he hollered or cried out, I couldn't tell you. Before I had time to even think about what I'd done, another explosion went off, bigger than the first one. I turned around and ran home as fast as I could.

It was dark by the time I made it back to the house, but I didn't go inside. I stuck my hand through the kitchen door and grabbed the keys to Daddy's truck off the key rack. I had to get Daddy's shine off our property before Maury and his cousin showed up to take it.

I loaded Daddy's truck with the four cases of whiskey from his hidey hole inside the henhouse and took off without discussing anything with him. I didn't want him to be held responsible for anything I'd done or was doing now.

None of this was his fault, it was all mine.

I thought about hiding the shine in Aunt Rosemary's and

Uncle Carl's root cellar. But I was afraid they might see me, and I'd have to tell them what was going on. I didn't want to tell them anything either. I was the one that started all this mess, I was the one who had to fix it.

I drove out to Old Mill Rd. before I could talk myself out of it. If anybody was going to make money off of Daddy's shine it would be my daddy. Not Maury or any of his yella belly cousins. Especially if they was going to mix it with their poison, not caring what happened.

Maury couldn't steal what we didn't have. As much as Daddy would hate what I was doing, I knew it was the right thing to do.

I pulled up to the front of the big white house, parking in the shadows behind the row of pecan trees that looked just like I'd imagined them. I went up and knocked on the door and stepped back into the shadows away from the porch light when it came on.

A man in a red flannel shirt stepped outside and let out a low whistle.

"Doggone it June, what happened to you?"

I'd not looked in a mirror, I was in such a hurry to get rid of the shine before Maury and Ferron stole it that I hadn't even thought about anything other than what I was doing right now.

"Why don't you come in and sit down, let my wife tend to that cut on your lip."

"I appreciate your concern, but I'm in a hurry."

I had to stop talking because I felt like I was going to start crying. If I started now, I might not be able to stop for a while. I guess I was in some kind of shock.

"Honey, let us help you." He said.

I steadied my voice and straightened my spine, "You want to help me? I've got four cases of my daddy's shine I want to sell. You want to help? Don't ask me any more questions, just buy them."

I saw the look on his face change from concern, to surprise, to the straight poker face he was known for. Jake's daddy had been trying to buy Daddy's shine for years.

"Pull on around to the barn over there and I'll send my son out to help you unload them while I get your money."

I was grateful he didn't ask any more questions. I needed to get back to the house before anything else happened. For all I knew, Ferron and Maury were there right now. Who knew how far they would go once they'd seen what I'd done.

I pulled up to the barn like he told me too and started to unload the cases without waiting for help. I heard someone beside me and about jumped out of my skin.

"It's okay, June. It's me, Jake." He slid a case out of the bed of the truck, and I followed him into the barn, glad for the darkness.

We were just setting the last two cases down when his father came in and handed me a roll of bills about the width of an ax handle.

"Here you go, forty a case. I thank you kindly. If you need help with anything, you know where to find me. And I mean anything, Ms. Fischer." I thanked him and hurried to the truck. Jake was right on my heels when I stepped out of the shadows.

"Whoa, June. Who did that you to you? I'll beat the living shit out of him." Jakes face was pale as a sheet and the muscles in his jaw bulged out. Any other day and I would've been happy to have his attention, but not like this. And not right now. Just thinking about his eyes on me made me queasy.

My foot slipped off the clutch as I tried to start the engine. I hadn't thought to check the gas gauge, and I hoped I had enough gas to get back home. My mind was flying all over the place, but Jake's voice brought me back.

"Where is he, June? Tell me and I'll go right now."

"You don't have to worry about it Jake, the person that did this won't never touch anybody else again." My voice sounded hard as red oak, but Jake didn't flinch or look away.

"June, I'm not sweet on Ellie like everybody thinks." Jake put his hands on the open window of the door and squeezed the metal until his knuckles turned white. "Can I call on you?"

I found the clutch and and turned the ignition, while I listened to Jake through my window. I couldn't believe my ears and couldn't figure out why he would say that to me right now. What did it even mean? I took a long hard look at him and wondered why his attention had seemed so important to me before. And what did he mean by asking if he could call on me? Why would he ask me now? Wasn't it clear I had other things on my mind? I was tired of trying to figure out what everybody else wanted.

It was time I figured out what *I* wanted.

"I don't know. I've got a lot on my mind. How about I call you if or when I figure it out?" I said and I peeled out of his driveway leaving him standing in the dust.

181

I was back home in less than an hour with only one small problem.

I'd passed somebody out on Talbet Road. I said a silent prayer that whoever it was would keep their mouth shut. Everybody knew my daddy's truck and it wasn't like him to be out so late unless something was wrong. It wouldn't take much before people came to the wrong conclusion once the news of the explosion got out.

I went inside, full of guilt and shame, expecting Daddy to be sitting at the table waiting for an explanation about where I'd been. But the kitchen was empty, and I heard Daddy's voice coming from their bedroom. He was talking to Mama the way he did when she had a spell, which explained why they weren't waiting up for me. She hadn't had a spell in a long time. I wondered if I'd caused it, if she sensed what I was feeling, and the thought hurt.

"Junebug, that you?"

"Yes, Daddy, it's me," I answered.

"Any luck?"

I had been lucky, that was for sure. Before I could answer he called out again.

"We going to have venison tenderloin for breakfast?"

"No Daddy, I didn't see any deer." I said to the closed door.

"Well dang, I thought for sure you'd gotten one. You were gone a long time, everything okay?"

"Everything's good, Daddy. I just lost track of time." The lie slid out of my mouth before I even had time to think about it. "I'm gonna wash up before turning in, I feel really dirty"— which wasn't a lie— "I'll see ya'll in the morning."

Suddenly, I was too tired to even think. I'd confess in the morning once Mama was feeling better.

Tears welled in my eyes, and when I reached up to wipe them away I flinched. My entire face felt like one big bruise. I went into the bathroom and couldn't believe the face that was looking back at me from the mirror. It didn't look like me in any way.

My lips were busted and swollen. There was dried blood from my nose and mouth smeared all over my chin and up in my hair. I had one black eye already and the other one was swollen almost shut—I imagined it'd be a nice shade of purple in the morning. My left ear was puffed-up and hot feeling and I had a cut on the back of my head. I didn't cry until I noticed the raised purple and red whelps on my throat from the leather belt that had been used to choke me. They were too sore to touch.

That's when it hit me how close I'd come to being forced to almost give myself to that man and being left for dead out in the woods. It hit me how fast everything can change.

I'd left my house an innocent fifteen-year-old girl who still didn't know how to kiss right and had come back a murderer.

I let the water run in the sink to hide my sobs and did the best I could to get the dried blood out of my hair, but I couldn't make myself take off my bloody clothes. I couldn't get past the second button on my blouse.

Before I turned in, I got Daddy's shotgun down from the rack above the mantle. I usually didn't like the feel of it, but to-night was different. Tonight I liked the weight.

I sat up all night in my room with the shotgun on my lap,

both barrels loaded. I had a clear view of the road through one window and view of the henhouse through the other one. I turned off my light before settling in so when Maury and Ferron came they wouldn't know I was watching. I hid the money I'd been given under my mattress and tried not to think about my great granddaddy sitting in his jail cell all those years ago. I'd never met him, he was buried before I was born, but I'd heard stories. I wonder if he ever felt as guilty as I did. I wonder if he'd ever killed anybody or if I was the first true outlaw in the family.

A few times I almost fell asleep, but when I closed my eyes I could see Maury's daddy on top of me and hear him telling me he was going to give me what I wanted, then I'd hear Maury telling me I didn't know what I wanted…

Well – I knew what I didn't want, that was for damn sure. I didn't want to see his car coming up our drive. If Maury and that low life came, they'd be sorry. Mr. Graves's death had been an accident, but I was pretty sure I could shoot Maury and Ferron on purpose.

But no one came and I watched the sun coming up over the rise. I closed my eyes for just a minute while I waited for the smell of coffee to let me know Daddy was awake. I woke up to a knock at the door and saw the sheriff's car through my window.

Whoever I'd passed on Talbet Road had to have told the sheriff they saw Daddy's truck. The sheriff must've been called to Shale and then put two and two together. I leapt to my feet and put my ear to the door to hear what was being said.

When I heard Sheriff Bailey ask Daddy where he'd been last night, I yanked the door open and rushed out into the parlor with the shotgun still in my hand. I'd forgotten about the bruises and cuts on my face and arms because honestly I didn't feel anything; I was numb all over. The looks on their faces reminded me and I knew I had to look a sight.

"What in the … June?" Daddy started towards me.

The sheriff's deputy stepped between us and raised his hand to my chin but decided not to touch me. He must've seen something in my eyes that told him not to. He reached for the gun instead and calmly took it out of my shaking hands.

"Mam, what happened to you?" the deputy asked.

"You don't need to be bothered with that. All you need to know is two things. Number one—I blew up that still. I did it, by myself. Nobody was supposed to get hurt. Or killed. That was an accident. Purely coincidental." I was almost yelling, but I didn't care. I just needed to talk.

"Junebug…", Daddy took a step closer to me, but I held up my hand. If he were to try and hug me, I would've started crying.

I took a deep breath and continued, "Number two—I ran Daddy's shine out of here. I did it, not my daddy. Just me." I looked at Daddy and hoped he'd forgive me. "He didn't know nothing about it."

The sheriff took his hat from his head and twirled it around in his hands as he looked at the floor. He put it back on, took a deep breath and rubbed his eyes. I couldn't stand the silence.

"That's why you come by, ain't it?" I yelled. The way he was rubbing his eyes made me feel like he didn't believe me. "You said you had to ask my daddy something. Well, Daddy don't know anything about it. He's innocent. It was all me …"

185

The sheriff put his hand up to stop me from talking. "June, you hold on a second. Okay? Just hold up. I think you might have a concussion and I don't think you're thinking clearly. I want you to listen close while I tell you why I'm here, and then I want you to tell me who hurt you."

He was talking real slow like he was speaking to a small child. "June. I came by to ask your daddy when was the last time he saw Lonnie Hinkle. We found him dumped in a ditch off Possum Trot Road. Somebody gave him some bad moonshine."

"My daddy don't make bad ..." I stopped. I'd forgotten all about Lonnie. "Is he dead?"

"No. He's gonna live but..." the deputy looked at the sheriff and stopped talking.

"I wasn't here to ask if your daddy did it, I know your daddy didn't do it. I just wanted to ask him if he had any idea who did. That was all."

"Well, you need to be asking me, not Daddy. I know where that man named Lonnie got the whiskey from, but you don't have to worry about that still anymore. I blew it up," I looked at daddy, "on accident."

No one said a word and I stood there waiting for him to put handcuffs on me.

The sheriff took his hat off once again and looked at daddy. "Randall, could I have a cup of that coffee? I need to clear my head. I think we all do."

"Ya'll come on in the kitchen." Daddy took my hand, his eyes filled with water and his hands shook, but his voice was steady. "Junebug, honey, come have a seat. I need to tend to that

186

lip of yours."

I hadn't noticed that it had started bleeding again. I touched my lip and looked at the bright red blood on my fingertips. I'd been strong up to that point, but I wasn't sure how much longer I could keep from crying.

We went into the kitchen and Daddy poured the coffee. The sheriff put his hat on the table and took off his badge. He laid it inside his hat. The deputy took his badge off and tossed it on top of the sheriff's.

"June, who did this to you?"

Daddy couldn't keep quiet any longer. "I'll kill that son of a bitch, Mau—"

"Daddy, it wasn't him. It wasn't Maury. It was his daddy. But you don't have to worry about him, because he's dead." I cried then, and they let me while Daddy got a washcloth and some cool water for my face.

"June, I know it ain't easy, but tell us everything that happened."

So I did. I told the whole sordid tale, from the first time I saw Maury and how he seemed awfully interested in my daddy, that embarrassing first date, and driving by Maury's house and seeing his daddy whip his mama with his belt. I put my hand to my throat when I thought of that and I saw how the deputy and the sheriff looked at each other. The way the deputy grit his teeth I was afraid he would break them off.

I told them about overhearing Maury and his cousin Ferron talking about getting ahold of Daddy's shine and cutting it with theirs. Then I told them how I had snuck up on the ridge and how

I'd seen Lonnie drunk, blind, and crippled being put into a truck by Maury and Ferron. I took a deep breath and told them the rest. I spilled my guts, not leaving anything out, up to the minute I fired the last arrow.

"I don't know why it blew up. I never expected that to happen. It doesn't make sense." Then I remembered the cans of kerosene they'd taken out of the back of the truck. How close they'd been to the fire. It didn't matter at that point, did it? None of it would've happened if I hadn't gone up there snooping around. I caused it all.

"I'm sorry…"

Before I could say anything else, the sheriff cleared his throat and said directly to me. "June, I'm sorry we weren't there to protect you. That's my duty, but it sounds like you did a damn fine job of that yourself. I'm proud of you. You have nothing to be sorry for, not one damn thing."

The deputy took his badge from the sheriff's hat but didn't pin it back on. He started to say something but stopped. Instead he tipped his hat to me. The sheriff stood and put his badge and hat back on. He stretched his shoulders and neck, taking a minute before he spoke.

"Well, I appreciate you both for the hospitality. I reckon me and Kimbro need to go see about a still that may have blown up over in Shale. Ya'll hadn't heard anything about that have you?"

I was puzzled, but Daddy put his arm around my shoulder and looked down at me.

"No, I didn't think you did. Probably some idiot making rot gut blew himself up. Happens all the time. I'm pretty sure that's what we'll find once we get over there. I'd bet my badge on it."

He nodded slightly and looked around our kitchen like he was searching for something.

"Oh, I almost forgot why I came by, Randall. I knew you had a few concerns about a young man that was harrassing your daughter. I wanted to let you know that you and your daughter won't be bothered by that Maury Graves character anymore. We've gotten information from a reliable source that he was selling tainted whiskey and he's wanted for questioning in the attempted murder of Lonnie Hinkle."

Whew, I'm parched! How about a glass of tea?

I told you it was a doozy. It might not be the story you wanted, but it's my story and it's all true.

Sheriff Bailey caught up with Maury and he confessed the whole thing. Maury and Ferron were charged with attempted murder. They went easy on Maury since he didn't have any prior convictions, but that boy never could keep his mouth shut and got himself shot and killed by one of his cousins before he served any time. And his daddy? Well, nobody seemed to even wonder what happened. Sheriff Bailey told us that the whole clan of Graves' had been trying to kill each other for years and if I hadn't caused him to blow himself up, he'd have died some other way soon enough.

Daddy wouldn't take the money Jake's daddy gave me from the sale of his shine. He insisted I spend it on myself. That started me thinking about going off to school, but I didn't know what I'd study for. I went back and forth for a while and finally bought myself a bandsaw and started making furniture alongside Daddy. Wasn't too long until he turned the whole thing over to me. I made a comfortable life for myself, doing something I loved and was my own damn boss to boot.

Me and Jake, well we had ourselves some fun. Once we'd both grown up and become adults. I didn't want to get married or have any younguns so after a while we parted ways. He ended up marrying Ellie after all. They had a whole mess of red-headed kids and seemed to be right happy. We actually became friends, Ellie and me. Good friends too. Her kids and grands and the great grands call me Aunt Bug. Now, ain't that something?

Lord, life is full of surprises!

Hell, I ain't dead yet. There's still some things I want to do before I expire.

What would an old woman like me possibly want to do?

Well, I don't rightly know, I'm still wondering about that myself. But I can tell you one thing, and it's the God's honest truth, I'll never need a man to tell me what it is.

# Cussing Snakes
# and Candy Cigarettes

*"That was God talkin' to you honey!
Did you listen? Did you hear?"*

I met my aunt the summer I turned ten.

I'll never forget the first time I laid eyes on her, walking through the headstones of the cemetery at my parents' private service. I'd mistaken her for Mama's ghost, which wasn't a far stretch for a ten year old child's imagination since my aunt was my mama's identical twin sister. I'd thought to myself that Mama had never looked so beautiful or so relaxed. She was walking barefoot in the grass like my alive mama would never do, the curls in her hair a soft, shiny tangle instead of chemically straightened and untouchable. Her freckles, free to breathe without the pancake makeup they usually hid under, made her look younger. My heart skipped when she started walking towards us, then took off at a gallop when my grandmother noticed her too.

But when Mama Kate called out, "Hello, Corrine," my stomach twisted. I was embarrassed for being so childish and hit with a feeling of guilt. Mama would've hated that I'd mistaken the heathen runaway for her.

She'd never had one good thing to say about her sister.

Corrine Margaret was a stranger, but she had been an obsession of mine. She was a fairytale character, similar to the troll in Billy Goat's Gruff or Rumpelstiltskin. Mama's identical evil twin who stole cars and lived in a box under a bridge, or worse in a commune full of weirdos and perverts in California. Half of my journal was filled with bits and pieces of information I'd picked up when Mama and her friends had one too many glasses of wine and moved out to the patio away from the men and their boring talk of politics and sports.

I would hide in my playhouse and eavesdrop with my pencil ready. Most of the time they talked about boring stuff, like who had plastic surgery or had gained weight, but when they started reminiscing about their high school days, the talk always went to Corrinne. She was equally terrifying and fascinating and made for great stories in my diary turned journal where I cast her as the villain in every single one.

I was thrown for a loop when Corrine smiled at me and reached for my chin. She wasn't scary at all, she smelled like lavender and fresh cut grass and her hands were soft and clean. Nothing at all like the hands I'd written about. She lifted my chin gently and looked at me like I was a person, a real person, and not a child. She inspected every inch of my face before she pinched my cheek and tugged gently on one of my unruly red curls.

"You are the spitting image of Charlie Thomas!"

Corrine had been the first person to mention him to me since the accident, and she didn't even whisper his name.

I was drawn to her like a moth to a candle.


In a strange twist of events I spent the summer with Corrine. My grandfather suffered a stroke just days after the funeral. Between all of the publicity from the accident—there was alcohol involved, a fact they tried to keep from me but was in the newspapers and on every local channel—and taking care of her husband, Mama Kate needed help. Corrine was the only living relative I had.

Once I got over my initial fear (we stayed in the house that had belonged to my other grandmother and not in a cardboard box under a bridge like I'd expected) I realized everything I'd heard about her was wrong.

Cory, she said no one called her Corrine, had more friends than anyone I'd ever met. The biggest contradiction to the stories I'd heard about her. They way Mama had talked about her, she was mean and hateful, and no one liked her. That was not true at all. We couldn't go anywhere that someone didn't stop her to say hello and tell her they were glad to see her back in Tennessee. She had friends in all colors, shapes, and sizes—men and women both. Mama and her small group of friends all looked alike. They even dressed in the same outfits and had their hair done in the same style. I hadn't thought anything of it before, because my friends and I dressed alike in our private school uniforms and were, I realized, all the same color too.

My life was turned upside down that summer, but Aunt Cory came to the rescue. She opened my eyes and taught me many valuable lessons. Like how to play and be a kid. She taught me not to judge other people and not take life so seriously. She taught me that rumors and gossip are more than words, they're actual physical things that can ruin someone's life. Or maybe, I learned that one on my own when I started writing new stories in my journal.

We all have a story. I realized after the night of the tent revival, Aunt Cory's story was better than anything I could make up and probably more exciting than any rumor I'd heard.

My new friends and I noticed posters and flyers tacked up in the windows for a revival at the corner drug store. It was our favorite place to go after a game of kickball for candy cigarettes, wax lips, and vanilla cokes. Aunt Cory said that she and my mother used to go there after school, but I couldn't imagine it. I'd never stepped foot in a place like the drug store before. But then again, I'd never played kickball, run barefoot through sprinklers, or made my own friends either. Up until then, any free time had been filled with scheduled activities and lessons. Things I did with the children of Mama's friends while they went to yoga or played tennis at the country club.

It had been months since Mama died, but I still worried about what she'd think as I slid the candy cancer sticks over the counter with my nickel. At first I wouldn't buy them, even when Kim teased me, and Pamela reminded me that my mama had died in a car wreck, not from lung cancer. But that wasn't the point, the point was my mama would be ashamed if she thought I was doing something so tacky as puffing on candy cigarettes. I knew she would hate it because she used to talk about anyone that smoked like they were white trash, even though she and her friends smoked on their Bunko nights and any other occasion they could sneak outside away from their husbands or spying kids.

I know because I used to watch them from my playhouse. But then again she would hate the fact that I didn't wear dresses every day, that I let my red curls go crazy and that I hadn't taken a piano lesson since I'd moved out of Mama Kate's big house. But what she would hate more than anything, is that we shopped at a store called Goodwill for most of my clothes. Mama had refused to wear, or dress me, in anything except the latest styles. She would go on shopping trips to Atlanta four times a year, and believe me, she had never stepped foot in a store that sold used items for anything, ever. Aunt Cory said it didn't make any sense to buy "play clothes" brand new, because they were supposed to get grass stained and worn out and it didn't even matter if they were boys' clothes as long as they were comfortable.

In the long run peer pressure won and I had a fake nicotine sugar habit with the rest of them, a pack a day no less. I loved the way my pink lip gloss left little circles on the candy butts which is another thing my mama would not have approved of. Only trashy girls wore lip gloss.

Aunt Cory told me I looked cute when I wore Pamela's bubblegum flavored Lip Smacker's gloss. She never told me I looked trashy, and she never said anything about the candy I bought except to ask me if I needed change to buy more. She was just happy I'd made friends and was having fun.

Pamela, Kim and I gulped our vanilla cokes and looked at the posters in the window.

"Boring." Kim said and then sucked the last bit of coke through her straw.

"Looks like a bunch of weirdos." Pamela said, as she finished her drink right behind Kim. She burped before yelling, "Last one to the softball field is a rotten egg!"

But I had half of my drink to finish so I used that as an excuse to stay behind and look at the posters. I couldn't stop thinking about the revival.

The posters for the revival read, "Calling all Preachers and Ministers." In my mind I pictured a bunch of preachers in all different sizes and shapes, dressed in tails and top hats.

"Welcome to the Greatest Show on Earth. Come on in and hear Ernie—the fastest preach in the South. Step on up, ladies and gentlemen and be blown away by our fat lady on the piano." I could see her, all five hundred pounds, dressed in a big flowery dress and huge floppy hat. Circles of pink rouge on her pretty white cheeks.

Would the choir be a group of acrobats? Would someone be juggling hymnbooks? Would there be cotton candy and popcorn? Would Aunt Cory go with me?

Aunt Cory was not a religious person at all. Mama had always referred to her as a heathen, but actually Cory was a very spiritual person when you got to know her. Always open to different opinions and the first one to help anyone in need. She sort of made up her religion as she went along. Basically be a good person and God (or whoever/whatever) would be happy with you and all would be right with the world. Treat people and animals the way you want to be treated and take care of those who can't take care of themselves. It worked for her, and I found myself thinking more like her every day. But I didn't dwell on that too much; we'd been Church of Christ to the core. Even if it was only on Sundays, Mama took it serious.

Anyway, Aunt Cory got all excited when she heard there would be snake handlers at the revival. She was fascinated by the whole thing and said she'd be happy to go with me.

When the big night finally came the two of us marched down to the big white tent that had been constructed for the revival.

I kept expecting to hear an elephant's trumpet or a lion's roar. There were lots of people there, and I assumed they traveled with the circus, um revival, because they all wore the same kind of uniform. Plaid shirts for the men, and long skirts for the women. It never crossed my mind that people would actually come there for religious reasons until we stepped inside the tent.

There was a lot of commotion going on. A lot of amens and

hallelujahs and stuff like that, people dancing and sweating and raising their arms up over their heads like they were reaching out to someone that only they could see. There were some people speaking in tongues, which I'd read about, but never seen. A few people fell out, I mean on the ground, right in the middle of the aisles. I could feel something in the air, it was very exciting and I couldn't wait to get back and write it all down.

My aunt took my hand and gave it a squeeze. I looked up at her and she grinned at me.

"This is a little different than your regular Sunday school class, huh, Chickpea?" she giggled.

"Yes, ma'am." I answered.

I went to church on Sunday because Mama would've wanted me to, and, honestly I liked it. It was something constant and steady in my life, which I needed after so many surprises. Even though I left there with more questions than answers after the death of my parents. The only answers I seemed to get from my Sunday school teachers were that I asked too many questions for someone my age. Aunt Cory wasn't much help either. She had a sticker on her guitar case that read "Eve Was Framed". So as you can imagine, the list of questions was never ending.

Sometimes Cory walked me to church, but she never went inside, not even after the preacher came out on the sidewalk to personally invite her in. Instead she lit a cigarette, blew a smoke ring and told him that she didn't need to be born again, she felt she got it right the first time.

The preacher didn't seem insulted. Instead he'd grinned at me and patted my head as he passed to go back inside. Mama would've had a fit, but I was proud to be Cory's niece, even if she was an outlaw. I'd never met anyone who said what they meant, except for Mama Kate. But Mama Kate never cussed.

Through all the commotion going on around us, we saw a man up front holding some mean looking snake. The snake was huge, wrapping his tail around the man's forearm and sticking his face out over the crowd, then back towards the man like he was trying to figure out who to bite first. I blinked and realized the man actually had two of them and was holding another snake up over his head. It was so weird, I don't know if I can really describe it. This man looked crazy and perfectly sane all at the same time. He was sweating something awful, but he seemed to be cool as a cucumber.

I turned to Cory to say something but forgot the words when I saw her face. Cory watched him and I watched her watch him and I knew  something was about to happen. I could feel it all the way to the marrow of my bones. She stood up, squeezed my hand hard and then let it go. I watched as my aunt walked down the middle of the aisle, stepping over people as she made her way to the front. She never took her eyes off the snake the man was holding over his head.

She walked up to the first row of folding chairs and stopped.

I could see Cory clenching and unclenching her fists, but I couldn't see her face. I wanted to see her better, so I moved out in the aisle, taking care not to stop on anyone as I went.

The crazy sane man holding the snakes noticed her and they stared at each other without speaking. He nodded and Cory took a couple of steps closer. The man danced a little jig, and I knew he felt the same thing I felt coming from her and it sparked something in him. He smiled at her and Cory stepped even closer.

I felt like I was in a dream. It looked like Cory was talking to the snake—I thought I could hear her voice, but her mouth wasn't moving. I couldn't make out any words, but it seemed like the snake could. It was staring right at her, like he was heeding every word that her eyes conveyed.

I walked down the aisle as close to her as I dared. There were some weird smells inside that tent. I'd always been overly sensitive to smells, but I'd never smelled anything like that before. I stood there and wondered selfishly what I would do if I lost my aunt to a snakebite. Before my Aunt Cory, my life had been so boring…and fake. Like the campaign ads for Daddy's gubernatorial election that he hated, but Mama loved. I realized at that moment I loved my aunt and I would be lost without her.

Then something unbelievable happened. The man held the snake out to her, and I swear she took it. She just reached out and took it! Holding the snakes' head between her thumb and middle finger in a firm grip, she raised it up to her face. She brought it up to an inch away from her freckled nose and looked it square in the eye. I was sure it had hypnotized her.

I could see her face and I was hit with a different scent, I could smell fear coming off of her in waves. It smelled strange, like vinegar and lemon and something else. But it was her fear, I am sure of it, coming up and over all the other smells around me. She stared that snake down and the scent faded somewhat.

Then she smiled a confident smile and said, "Fuck you."

I almost died from the thrill of it—we were in a church for crying out loud! My aunt had just dropped the worst curse word ever right there in front of God and everybody. Even if it was a tent and there was a fat lady (minus the rouge and the floppy hat) playing the piano, it was still a religious event. Thank goodness the lady at the keyboard banged away on the keys, because the crazy man with the snakes didn't hear my aunt with all of the racket going on around us.

Snakes or no snakes, I don't think he would have approved.

I watched my aunt stare down that snake until the smile faded from her face, making her look like a lost child. Cory didn't look like Cory when she wasn't smiling. She handed the snake back to the handler just as easy as you would pass a saltshaker to a dinner guest, and stepped back without one single bite, thank god. When he took it from her I realized her hands were shaking something terrible.

Someone called out in a frantic voice, "That was God talking to you, honey! Did you hear? Did you listen?"

Cory turned to where the voice came from and found a lady with her hair coming out of her bun holding a bible over her head.

"Oh, hell—that wasn't God talking to me. No ma'am! Nowhere close to God. And, no, this time I didn't listen." She threw her head back and laughed, and I exhaled as the color came back to her cheeks.

"You ready to get out of here?" Cory asked when she reached me. I nodded and she took my sweaty, shaking hand in her own sweaty shaking hand. We walked past all those odd people and their strange smells out into the fresh air.

"Cory, were you really talking to that snake?"

"Him? Oh yeah, he was an ex-husband of mine. He was a snake back then, too. I always wanted to tell him that," She let go of my hand, stretched both arms up over her head and yawned, "but I never got the chance."

She looked up at the moon like nothing had happened. Seeing her like that, arms stretched, yawning – relaxed and at ease, you would never have guessed that just minutes ago, she'd cussed a snake in the middle of a sermon.

A snake that was an ex-husband, no less.

She put her arm around my shoulders and gave me a squeeze.

"How did you know he was going to be here?"

Cory looked confused, then raised her eyebrows and shrugged with a grin.

"I didn't."

Once Mama Kate and my Grandfathers' lives were back to normal, Aunt Cory and I would go back to normal too. That meant I'd move back to the big house and private school, and Aunt Cory would leave Tennessee. The thought of her leaving almost made me cry.

Cory was so much more than the gossip and rumors that had been handed back and forth, stretched and warped to fit other people's stories. She might be a little bit crazy, but she didn't try to hide it. She was the most honest person I'd ever met. I sure was going to miss her.

I had no idea how to put all that into words, so instead of speaking, I pulled out my pack of candy Lucky Strikes from the pocket of my sweater and offered one to her.

"We'll have to get you on a sugar patch to help you kick this disgusting habit before we send you back to Mama Kate." Cory said as she patted my upper arm. "Unless you want to come home with me to New Orleans…"

She pulled an imaginary lighter from her cleavage and leaned down to light the ends of our cigs and I felt something pass between us. She winked before she reached for my hand, and we walked the rest of the way home in silence.

No need to speak the words out loud, because we felt them rise and swirl with the sugar smoke rings we blew under the light of the full moon as we made our way home.

## Acknowledgements

I want to thank Suzanne Hudson and her husband, Joe Formichella, who opened up there home on Waterhole Branch and gave me a place to stay when I was promoting my first collection. They threw a Grits and Gumbo get together to introduce me and Walking to a great group of people, and gave me advice and a pep talk before my book event at Page and Palette. I don't know how I got so lucky, but I damn sure did.

Suzanne critiqued these stories and gave me her honest to god opinions. I listened to some of them. If you don't like these stories, don't blame her. I'm hardheaded and stubborn, but I think that's why we get along so well-she's possibly more ornery than me. But if you do like them, it's because she pushed me to make them better. I did take that advice. Thank you Suzanne for not letting me be a slacker.

I want to thank Sonny Brewer for sharing his birthday with me at Page and Palette Bookstore in Fairhope, Alabama. I also want to thank Sonny and his dog Bobby for their advice, friendship, and for reminding me that life is full of miracles.

Susan Cushman, I don't know how you found time to read this while you were knee deep in research and writing every day on your novel, but I am so very thankful that you did. Thank you for your encouragement and keen eye.

Thanks to everyone who read the stories in Walking the Wrong Way Home and asked for more, to you that read these stories and encouraged me to publish them, and to everyone who preordered a copy. Thank you kindly.

Laura Covino-aka the Mudge-thank you for your blue ink

marks, beer, and musings from your porch.

And thank you Pamela Lambiase for the phone calls reminding me who I am and what I'm doing.

The world was thrown for a loop due to Covid-19. So many plans were changed and put on hold. Lives were turned upside down and sideways but hopefully we'll get through it together.

Please stay safe, healthy, and as sane as possible - and I hope my stories help pass the time while we wait for things to get back to normal.

Thank you for reading – I'd be lost without you.

xo

*Some praise for Walking the Wrong Way Home:*

"*It may be fiction but it's all true. Mandy writes razor-sharp, down-to-the bone southern tales about total strangers that you've known your whole life. They jump off the page and grab you by the heart and they hang on long after the words have stopped. She knows us better than we know ourselves. This is the good stuff-get you some!*"- **Mike Henderson, Grammy award winning singer/songwriter, musician, and all around badass**

"*I loved these stories and the way that they reveal their truth with the slow, meticulous precision of a surgeon. This writer is not afraid to cut deep to reveal hidden truths and deliver justice in surprising ways the reader doesn't see coming. Mandy Haynes is inventive, original and Southern to the bone.*" **River Jordan, author of Confessions of A Christian Mystic, Southern Writers on Writing *, Praying for Strangers, The Miracle of Mercy Land, Saints In Limbo, The Messenger of Magnolia Street, The Gin Girl**

"*With the spirit of a barefoot, callous-kneed tomboy lifting stones to collect grubs, beetles, and wiggle worms for creek-fishing, Mandy Haynes never averts her eyes or shies away from the hard truths of rough living. She's casting into the weeds, where silt-dwellers and mud bugs are circled by dragonflies, their brilliant sapphire blues and the lace of their wings darting and emerging, like Haynes' tales, from all six directions, and with redemptive grace.*"-**Suzanne Hudson, prize winning author of 2018's Shoe-Burnin' Season: A Womanifesto (pseudonym R.P. Saffire) and 2019's The Fall of the Nixon Administration, a comic novel**